True or False

Elizabeth led Amy to a circle of chairs where they could continue their conversation in private. "I've been talking to Jessica, and she says that Sam is always bragging."

"She sure is. You should have heard her yesterday at lunch. She even said her family has a house in Hawaii."

Elizabeth leaned forward. "Well, Jessica thinks Sam is making up most of her stories."

"I had the same suspicion," Amy admitted. "I even asked Sam why she hadn't written me about all the stuff she's been talking about, but she just said she had forgotten to."

"Jessica is going to try to prove that Sam is lying," Elizabeth said bluntly.

Amy's eyes opened wide. "How?"

Briefly Elizabeth explained.

"Wow. That would be great," Amy said, her eyes glowing. She glanced over in Sam's direction. "As far as I'm concerned, Samantha Williams deserves to be put in her place."

SWEET VALLEY TWINS

Amy's Pen Pal

Written by
Jamie Suzanne

Created by
FRANCINE PASCAL

A BANTAM SKYLARK BOOK®
NEW YORK · TORONTO · LONDON · SYDNEY · AUCKLAND

RL 4, 008–012

AMY'S PEN PAL

A Bantam Skylark Book / January 1990

Sweet Valley High® *and Sweet Valley Twins are trademarks of*
Francine Pascal

Conceived by Francine Pascal

Produced by Daniel Weiss Associates, Inc., 33 West 17th Street,
New York, NY 10011

Cover art by James Mathewuse

Bantam Books are published by Bantam Books, a division of Bantam
Doubleday Dell Publishing Group, Inc. Its trademark, consisting of
the words "Bantam Books" and the portrayal of a rooster, is Registered
in U.S. Patent and Trademark Office and in other countries. Marca
Registrada. Bantam Books, 666 Fifth Avenue, New York, New York 10103.

PRINTED IN THE UNITED STATES OF AMERICA

O   0 9 8 7 6 5 4 3 2 1

Amy's Pen Pal

One

◇

"Wow! What a great-looking sweater!" Jessica Wakefield pointed to a purple sweater prominently displayed in the store window.

Her twin, Elizabeth, tugged at her arm. "Come on, Jess. We didn't come to the mall to look at clothes."

"I'd really like to wear that to Lila's party tomorrow night," Jessica said thoughtfully.

Elizabeth sighed. Sometimes it was hard to get Jessica moving. "It *is* nice, but you already have so much purple," she said. At that moment, she caught sight of their reflections in the store window. Both girls had the same bright blue-green eyes, long, blond hair, and pretty, tanned faces. They were identical, right down to the dimples in their left cheeks. Only their expressions were different. Jessica was staring dreamily at the sweater, while Elizabeth was frowning.

Elizabeth stood up a little straighter. "Jessica, your big sister is ordering you to get moving."

Jessica made a face. "You're *only* four minutes older," she protested, turning away from the window. "I hardly think that makes you my big sister."

Elizabeth didn't answer. Usually the twins joked about those four minutes, but sometimes Elizabeth thought those four minutes were more like four years. No matter how much the two girls looked alike, their personalities were quite opposite.

Elizabeth was the more serious, responsible twin, while Jessica was always on the lookout for fun. Not that Elizabeth didn't know how to enjoy herself, but she found working on the school newspaper, *The Sweet Valley Sixers*, or reading to be much more exciting than talking about boys or clothes. Jessica lived for the minute and liked hanging around with fellow members of the Unicorn Club, an exclusive group made up of the most popular girls at Sweet Valley Middle School.

"It's not fair," Jessica grumbled as she followed Elizabeth down the escalator. "I really need a new sweater."

"Need?" Elizabeth raised her eyebrows.

Jessica started to laugh. Her fondness for clothes was a family joke.

"All right, I guess I do have a *few* things I could wear. But *you* haven't had anything new in a while, Lizzie," Jessica mused. "Maybe Mom would let you buy it—"

"And then you could borrow it," Elizabeth finished for her. "No way. I don't even need a new sweater."

"But, Lizzie . . ."

Elizabeth thought it was time to change the subject. "Don't you think we should go to Odds and Ends and see what kind of paper plates they have there?"

Jessica sat down on a bench in the center of the mall. "They had a perfectly good selection over at The Mart. I don't know why we didn't just buy those."

"They were all right, but Mom told us to

get something really nice. It's not everyday we throw a big barbecue."

"Giant barbecue," Jessica corrected. "Mom and Dad's friends, Steven's, and ours. It's going to be really crowded."

"This whole holiday weekend is full," Elizabeth agreed. "Tomorrow there's Lila's party; Sunday we have to help set up for the barbecue; Monday *is* the barbecue—"

"And don't forget Monday night," Jessica said, her eyes sparkling.

Elizabeth shook her head. "How could I forget when you've been talking about it all week? Dave Carlquist is broadcasting his radio show right here from the Valley Mall."

"And not just any show," Jessica reminded her. "They're going to be announcing the winner of the contest!"

Dave Carlquist was a high school senior whose radio show was the talk of Sweet Valley. He had a deep, soothing voice that all the girls loved, especially Jessica. Until now, his show had been broadcast from the high school facilities, but starting the following week, it was going to air on the local radio station. It would be a mixture of music and interviews, and to kick off the new program, they were holding a contest to see who could come up with the best name for the show. Elizabeth knew that Jessica had sent in at least ten entries.

" 'Teen Talk,' " Jessica said, savoring the words. "Don't you think that's a good one?"

Elizabeth didn't have the heart to tell her twin that she thought the name was boring. She hoped for Jessica's sake that one of her other suggestions was a little livelier. Since she loved playing around with words, Elizabeth had sent in an entry of her own, even though she wasn't very interested in the prize—a party at the new teen dance club, Jupiter, with music played by none other than Dave Carlquist.

The sounds of an electric saw interrupted Elizabeth's thoughts. "What's that?" she asked, looking around.

Jessica quickly surveyed the mall. "I think I know," she said, spotting a group of workmen setting up a large podium. "They must be building the broadcast booth." Her eyes sparkled with excitement.

Before Elizabeth could say anything, Jessica was pulling her toward the structure.

Sure enough, behind a roped-off area where

the workmen were sawing and hammering, there was a large poster that said:

Monday Night
Live From the Sweet Valley Mall
Deejay DAVE CARLQUIST!

"Do you think he's here somewhere?" Jessica asked, craning her neck.

"Why should he be?"

"Maybe he wants to check things out," Jessica replied.

"Do you know what he looks like?" Elizabeth asked.

Jessica shook her head. "No. But he's got such an awesome voice. I'm sure I'd know him if I saw him. He's probably tall, and really good-looking—"

Elizabeth's laugh interrupted her sister's daydreaming. "Or short, with really goofy glasses—"

"Don't be silly," Jessica said crossly. "Anyone who sounds like that has got to be gorgeous."

"Well, maybe," Elizabeth answered diplomatically.

"And when he announces my name as the winner of the contest, it will be the most exciting moment of my life."

"Let's get those paper plates, OK, Jess?"

Jessica looked around once again. There didn't seem to be anyone in the area who could possibly be Dave Carlquist. But she still didn't feel like walking all the way to Odds and Ends, which was on the other side of the mall. "Let's get something to eat first," she suggested.

"We had lunch just before we got here," Elizabeth pointed out.

"Then an ice cream."

"All right," Elizabeth agreed. Sometimes it just wasn't worth the effort to say no to her twin.

The twins headed for Casey's Place, an old-fashioned ice cream parlor that was popular among the middle schoolers. When they walked in, Jessica noticed several members of the Unicorn Club sitting at a corner table. Each of them was wearing something purple, the Unicorns' club color.

"Come on, Elizabeth, let's go over and sit with Lila and the others."

Elizabeth didn't really want to go. The Unicorns weren't exactly her favorite girls. Mary Wallace was nice, but the president of the club, Janet Howell, was stuck up, and Lila Fowler was the worst of all. The daughter of one of the wealthier men in town, Lila was a terrible snob. Elizabeth and her best friend, Amy Sutton, had often clashed with Lila.

"Can't we get our ice cream first?" Elizabeth asked.

But Jessica was already halfway to her friends' table. Elizabeth reluctantly followed behind her.

"Hi, Jessica," Lila called, flipping her brown hair over one shoulder. She gave Elizabeth a quick nod of recognition.

Jessica and Elizabeth crowded in at the small table. "Did you see the workmen building Dave Carlquist's booth?" Jessica asked excitedly.

"No," squealed Janet, a pretty girl with curly hair. "Where is it?"

"Over in the center of the mall."

"I wish Dave Carlquist was going to be the deejay at your party tomorrow night," Mary said to Lila.

"My father tried to get him," Lila said with a pout on her face, "but he was already booked."

"That's all right," Jessica said loyally. "It's going to be a great party anyway." Lila had invited almost everyone in the middle school.

"It certainly is. My dad hired this terrific caterer, and a new band, The Hot Heads."

"Are you coming to the party, Elizabeth?" Mary asked. Mary sometimes helped Elizabeth with the typing of *The Sweet Valley Sixers*.

"Yes, I'll be there." She had almost turned the invitation down, but Jessica had pleaded with her to come, telling her she would miss the party of the century if she didn't show up. After careful consideration, Elizabeth concluded it might be fun—even if Lila Fowler was the hostess.

"And what about Amy?" Lila said, rolling her eyes. She made no secret of her dislike for Elizabeth's friend.

"You'll have to ask her yourself," Elizabeth answered, trying to keep her voice level.

"Oh, I'm sure she'll be there," Janet said. "No one in her right mind would miss this party."

Lila took a final sip of her cola. "I have to finish shopping," she said. "I've got to find the perfect outfit for the party."

Elizabeth knew that Lila had even more clothes in her closet than Jessica. But her comment started a new round of chatter about what everyone was planning to wear.

Tapping Jessica's arm, Elizabeth whispered, "Let's go, Jess. We've got to get the plates and the decorations . . ."

Lila overheard Elizabeth. "Oh, you can't leave now, Jessica," she pleaded. "I really want you to look at a blouse I saw at Leslie's."

"Well . . ." Jessica glanced sideways at Elizabeth.

"And maybe we could look around for Dave Carlquist," Janet added. She clasped her hands to her chest and said in a theatrical voice, "Your true love."

Jessica laughed, but Elizabeth could tell the possibility of seeing Dave was a strong attraction.

"I suppose I could get the party stuff by myself," Elizabeth said slowly.

"Sure you can," Jessica exclaimed. "You're much better at that kind of thing than I am anyway."

Elizabeth got out of her seat. "OK, then, I'll see you later, Jess."

Jessica barely seemed to hear her. She was already deep in conversation with the other Unicorns, discussing whether or not Bruce Patman, the cutest boy in the seventh grade, would show up at Lila's party.

Elizabeth was used to Jessica going off with the Unicorns, so she didn't really mind shopping alone. When she entered Odds and Ends, she immediately spotted what she was looking for. Right next to the cash register were festive pink and green plates, matching cups, and a paper centerpiece that unfolded into an elaborate basket of flowers.

After she finished her shopping, Elizabeth hurried home. She burst into the Wakefields' house, eager to show off her purchases. But instead of finding her mother in the sunny kitchen, Amy Sutton was sitting at the table, eating a peanut butter sandwich.

"Amy, what are you doing here?" Elizabeth asked with surprise.

Amy swallowed a bite of food. "Waiting for you," she said.

"We weren't supposed to get together this afternoon, were we?" Elizabeth asked, suddenly worried.

"Nope. I thought I was going to the museum with my mother, but she had to work."

Elizabeth put her package down and took a seat across from Amy. "Isn't she working on some big project?"

"There's a broadcasting convention next weekend and my mother's running it," Amy confirmed. Mrs. Sutton was a television reporter for a local station. "She's got a lot of planning to do. So I got bored and came over here. Your mom insisted that I have a snack while I waited for you."

"That sounds like her," Elizabeth said with a grin. "Where is she now?"

Amy giggled. "There was a potato crisis."

"What?" Elizabeth exclaimed.

"Your mother was making potato salad, and she ran out of potatoes. She told me to wait for you while she went to the store."

Elizabeth's gaze wandered over to the mountain of potatoes piled high on the kitchen counter. "She needs more?" Elizabeth asked in amazement. "That looks like enough to feed an army." Elizabeth heard heavy footsteps coming down the stairs. "Or Steven," she added, as her brother burst into the room.

Steven Wakefield was a freshman at Sweet Valley High, and well-known for his huge appetite.

"Or Steven, what?" he said, opening the refrigerator door. After a quick survey, he grabbed a leftover piece of pie, heaped some whipped cream on it, and plunked himself down next to the girls.

"I was just saying I don't know who eats more, the population of a small city, or you."

"Very funny," Steven said, not the least bit upset. This kind of teasing was normal in the Wakefield household. And even though Steven could eat them out of house and home, and could be a big pain, both twins agreed that he was a pretty nice older brother—most of the time.

"How come you're home this afternoon?" Elizabeth asked. "I thought you'd be playing basketball or something."

"Not today," Steven said, wiping a bit of whipped cream off his chin. "I'm heading over to school."

"On a day off?" Elizabeth asked in disbelief.

"Is the school even open?" Amy asked.

"Just for the members of the radio club."

"He just joined the club," Elizabeth informed Amy.

"Some new equipment is arriving today. A couple of us want to get a look at it," Steven explained.

"I guess you want to be the next Dave Carlquist," Elizabeth said.

"Not me. He's got that deejay thing all sewn up. I just want to learn the board."

"What's the board?" Amy asked.

"That's what the controls in a radio studio are called," Steven explained. He pushed his empty plate away from him. "I'm going to be the man behind the deejay. And if I want to know what I'm doing, I'd better go look at that equipment. Have fun on your day off, squirts."

"Don't call us squirts," Elizabeth said, but Steven just laughed and waved goodbye. As soon as he was out the door, Elizabeth turned her attention back to Amy. "Do you have any plans for this afternoon?"

"Well," Amy began, looking embarrassed, "there is something I have to get done, and I wondered if you'd help me."

"That sounds interesting," Elizabeth said, leaning forward.

"Don't get your hopes up," Amy warned. "This is something I'd only ask of my best friend."

"I don't get it. What do you want me to do?"

Amy sighed. "Elizabeth, will you come over and help me clean up my room?"

Two

◇

Elizabeth laughed and then groaned.

Amy looked embarrassed. "My mother gave me strict orders to get my room cleaned up. She wants it spotless by tonight." Amy threw up her hands helplessly. "You've seen it. You know I could never do it all by myself."

Elizabeth did know. On its best days, the kindest way to describe Amy's bedroom was messy. And on its worst—well, she was sure the president could declare it a national disaster area.

"I know it's a big favor to ask," Amy said hesitantly.

"It's big, all right."

"But it would be so boring to do all that work alone."

Elizabeth laughed. "Gee, I'd hate to have you be bored while you're cleaning up your room," she teased.

"Pretty please?" Amy pleaded.

Elizabeth threw up her hands. "All right, all right. I have some time before dinner. I guess I can come over for a while."

"Elizabeth, you're a really good friend," Amy said sincerely.

"You'll do a favor for me someday," Elizabeth replied. She wagged her finger at Amy with mock seriousness. "And it will have to be a major one."

Elizabeth wrote her mother a note to tell her where she'd be, and left it on the kitchen counter where Mrs. Wakefield would be sure to find it. The two girls got on their bikes and started pedaling down the street.

"Which way do you want to go?" Elizabeth asked.

"Let's ride by the park," Amy answered.

"That's the long way. It will cut into our cleaning time."

"I just want to see if anyone is at the park."

"Anyone?" Elizabeth asked with mock suspicion.

Amy blushed. "Well, maybe Ken."

Amy and Ken Matthews liked each other, although they were both very shy.

"I want to see if he's going to Lila's party tomorrow," Amy murmured.

"All right," Elizabeth said agreeably, not wanting to embarrass her friend. "Let's get going."

As they pedaled down the street, the warm California sun shined down on them. The scent of freshly-bloomed flowers filled the air. It felt good to be out in the fresh air, even if it was just for a little while.

When they arrived at the park, it was filled with mothers and children enjoying the playground and older kids taking advantage of the day off from school.

Elizabeth pulled up alongside Amy, who had skidded to a stop and was scanning the park for Ken. "Do you see him?" she asked.

Amy shook her head. Suddenly she spotted two boys playing basketball. "Over there," she pointed.

"Yes, it's Ken and Patrick."

When the girls arrived at the edge of the basketball court, both boys looked up.

"Hi, Elizabeth, Amy," Patrick Morris said in a friendly voice. Patrick was a sixth grader at the middle school along with the others.

Ken tucked the ball under his arm. "What's happening?"

Amy, suddenly shy, didn't say anything. "We're just going over to Amy's," Elizabeth answered.

"Are you guys going to that party over at Lila's tomorrow night?" Patrick asked.

Amy, relieved that she didn't have to be the one to bring up the party, jumped into the conversation. "Yes, we are. What about you?"

Patrick shrugged. "Lila's not exactly one of my favorites, but I guess I might show up."

"I don't know why she bothered asking us," Ken said. "I thought she only wanted to hang around with guys like Bruce Patman."

Elizabeth knew that Ken didn't like Bruce any better than she did. Rich and good-looking, Bruce was just Lila's type. Elizabeth thought he was a conceited snob.

"I think she invited most of the kids just so she could impress them," Elizabeth said frankly.

"But from what she was telling us this afternoon, I guess it is going to be the event of the year." Quickly, Elizabeth filled the boys in on Lila's plans.

"It's sounding better," Ken said.

"Oh, you'd go anywhere for free food," Patrick teased.

Ken gave Patrick a small punch in the arm. "Look who's talking."

After chatting for a few more minutes, Elizabeth said, "Well, we'd better get going."

"Why? It's not that late," Ken said, looking at Amy.

Reluctantly, Amy answered, "Elizabeth is helping me with a little project this afternoon."

"You're not doing homework on the first day of a long weekend, are you?" Patrick asked.

The girls looked at each other. "No, we're just conducting a little investigation," Elizabeth finally said.

"Sounds mysterious," said Patrick.

"Yeah, well, see you later," Amy said. The girls hopped on their bikes and rode away.

When they were out of earshot, Amy and Elizabeth started laughing. "An investigation? How did you come up with that?" Amy asked, giggling.

"It wasn't a lie," Elizabeth said indignantly. "I'm sure once we clean a lot of that junk away, we'll make some real discoveries."

When they arrived at Amy's house and went up to her room, Elizabeth's worst fears were confirmed. There were so many things on Amy's unmade bed, it was hard to see the sheets. A broken kite was draped over a lampshade, and piles of clothes littered the floor like small hills.

"Where do we begin?" Amy said glumly.

Elizabeth was well-organized, but even she had to stop and think for a moment. "Why don't we put all the dirty clothes into the laundry hamper? Then we can see what's left."

"That's a good idea," Amy said. "Maybe I'll find something to wear to the party tomorrow." At Elizabeth's look of horror, she added, "After I wash it, that is."

With both Elizabeth and Amy working hard, things soon began to take shape. They brought all the dirty clothes down to the basement and put dozens of books back on their shelves.

"Well, it's starting to look like a room again," Elizabeth said, flopping down on the newly-made bed.

"Instead of a pigsty," Amy added. "I don't know why I let it get so bad."

Elizabeth felt something under the bed covers, and pulled out a crumpled candy wrapper. "Well, just remember all this work the next time you're tempted to drop something on the floor."

"Oh, I will," Amy said fervently. "I'm never going to let this place get so messy again."

Elizabeth reached over to a pile of papers sitting on the desk. She plucked one of them off the top and started reading. "Amy, what's this?" she asked.

Amy came over and sat next to Elizabeth. "It's the paper I did on the solar system last year," she said.

"How come you didn't throw it away?" she said.

Amy shrugged. "I don't know."

"Do you keep *everything*?"

"Almost everything," Amy said with a laugh. She grabbed the rest of the papers and started rifling through them. "Here's a note you sent me a couple of months ago."

"You could write the story of your life with all the things you keep!" Elizabeth declared.

Amy started to read a letter. "This is from my pen pal, Samantha Williams."

"How is Sam?"

"I don't really know. I haven't heard from her in ages. I'm starting to get worried. She used to write me at least once a month."

The shrill ring of the telephone interrupted their conversation. "I'll get it," Amy said, hurrying into the hallway where the phone sat. A minute later she poked her head back into the bedroom. "It's for you, Elizabeth. It's Jessica."

Elizabeth got up and took the phone from her friend. "What's up, Jess?"

"I thought I'd find you over there. What are you doing?"

"Helping Amy clean up her room."

Jessica groaned. "Lizzie, only you would spend a perfect afternoon doing chores. And they're not even yours!"

"We're almost done."

"Well, Mom wants you home. We're all going out to dinner at Juan's. Mom's so tired from preparing food for the barbecue, she says she wants to be waited on tonight."

Juan's was a new Spanish restaurant in town and the Wakefields had been planning to try it. "I'm leaving now," Elizabeth promised.

"Are you leaving?" Amy asked when Elizabeth reentered the room.

"Yes, but at least I was able to help you get a good start."

"You've done more than your share. I can take it from here."

After thanking Elizabeth and saying goodbye, Amy set about putting the rest of the room in order. She was making great strides until she remembered she had promised to phone her mother. Glancing at her watch, Amy realized her call was overdue.

Pulling the phone into the bedroom, Amy dialed her mother's office. The phone rang a long time before Mrs. Sutton answered.

"Oh, Amy, I'm so glad you called. I haven't had a moment to pick up the phone."

"Are you going to be home for dinner?" Amy asked hopefully.

"I'm sorry, darling, I can't. I have to go out with some clients. And Daddy's working late. Will you be all right?" Mrs. Sutton asked anxiously.

Amy was disappointed, but she tried to sound cheerful for her mother's sake. "Sure, there's plenty in the refrigerator."

"All right, then. I'll be home as soon as I can."

Amy looked around at the room. "Wait until you see how clean my room is."

Mrs. Sutton laughed. "I'm looking forward to that."

Amy replaced the receiver with a sigh. *Back to work,* she thought. But before she got started, the doorbell rang. "Who could that be?" Amy muttered as she ran downstairs.

She peeked through the front door window. Standing on the doorstep was a thin girl with red hair and freckles. She was carrying a suitcase. At first, Amy had no idea who she was. But when she realized, she flung open the door.

"Sam Williams!" she cried. "What in the world are you doing here?"

Three

◆

Sam gave a nervous little giggle. "Well, aren't you going to ask me inside?"

"Oh, sure," Amy replied quickly. "Come on in. I'm just so surprised to see you. It's a good thing you sent me that photo, or I never would have recognized you."

Sam stepped inside to the hallway and set down her suitcase. "It's hard to believe that we've never met. I feel like I know you so well."

An awkward silence followed while the girls stared at each other. Finally, Amy said, "It's so funny that you're here. I was telling my friend Elizabeth about you this afternoon."

"You were?"

"Yes. I found one of your letters, and I mentioned to her that it had been a long time since I'd heard from you."

"Well, things have been kind of crazy around my house lately. I—I did write you a letter saying I was coming for a visit." Sam looked embarrassed. "Didn't you get it?"

"No. This is a total surprise."

The silence fell again. Amy smiled awkwardly and said, "But I'm glad you're here."

"You are?" Sam asked hopefully.

"Of course. I've always wanted to meet you. Come on in."

Sam looked around warily. "Where are your parents?"

"Oh, they're both at work. They're going to be late tonight."

"Great!" Sam exclaimed. "Then we're on our own for a couple of hours."

"At least."

"I hope they won't be upset that I've turned up."

"Oh, no. They won't be." At least Amy hoped they wouldn't be. "Why don't you bring your suitcase upstairs? Then you can change, if you want to."

Glad that she had done her cleaning before Sam arrived, Amy led Sam upstairs to her room.

"Oh, it's pretty," Sam said, looking around.

"It wasn't a few hours ago," Amy confided. "I just did a huge cleanup."

"Do you hate to clean your room, too?"

"You bet." The girls smiled at each other. "Hey, how did you get here, anyway?" Amy asked. "Did you fly?"

"No, I took the train," Sam said. "Then I took a bus from the train station."

Amy made herself comfortable on the bed. "I can't believe you did that all by yourself. I can't even get around the block in a new city."

Sam shrugged. "It wasn't so hard."

"Do you want something to eat?" Amy asked. "I was just about to have dinner."

"That would be great!" Sam said. "I'm famished."

"Why don't you wash up, and I'll put a pizza in the microwave."

"Good idea." Sam got up and opened her suitcase. She pulled out a wrinkled plaid shirt and jeans. "I'll change and be right down."

Amy went downstairs and popped the pizza in the microwave. As she set the table, she thought about the amazing coincidence of Sam showing up. When Sam came into the kitchen, looking refreshed, Amy said, "Do you believe in ESP?"

Samantha looked thoughtful. "I don't know."

"Well, I think we have it. I mean, I was thinking about you and all of a sudden you appeared at my door."

Sam ran a hand through her curls. "It's strange, all right."

"And you picked the perfect weekend to come."

"I did?" Sam took a seat at the kitchen table.

"Yes," Amy replied, as she took the pizza out of the microwave. "We're off from school until next Tuesday, and there's tons of stuff going on in Sweet Valley this weekend."

"Like what?"

Amy filled Sam in on all the upcoming events: the barbecue, the radio show, and of course Lila's party.

Sam looked a little nervous. "Are you certain I won't be imposing? I mean, these people don't even know me."

"Well, the Wakefields won't mind having you over. Elizabeth is my best friend, and she's going to be thrilled you're here. She's heard all about you."

Sam took a bite of pizza. "But what about this party? Will Lila mind me coming uninvited?"

"No, it's going to be an enormous party. All of the Unicorns will be there and most of Sweet Valley Middle School, too."

"What are the Unicorns?"

"Didn't I write you about them? It's a club. A lot of the really popular girls in the middle school are in it."

"Are you?"

"No," Amy admitted. "They're kind of snobby."

"Oh, I see," Sam said knowingly. "There's a club like that at my school, too. The Rainbows."

"Do you belong?" Amy asked.

"No. We're not really interested in the same things."

"That's just how it is at my school," Amy agreed. "By the way, do you still have your horse?"

Sam took a sip of cola. "Sure. Little Bit is the best horse in the whole world. We've been entering a few horse shows."

"You have?" Amy asked, impressed. "Have you won any?"

"Not yet. But we're working on it."

"I've done a little riding, but nothing like you. Having a horse of your own has got to be the best."

For the next few minutes the girls talked about horses. Then Amy filled Samantha in on some of the other things she had been doing, including working on *The Sweet Valley Sixers*.

"I'd like to work on the newspaper at my school," Sam said. "Maybe you could show me some copies of yours."

"Sure," Amy said, and she ran upstairs to get the latest issues. The girls went through them carefully, with Amy pointing out some of the stories she had written. When they finished eating, Amy said, "It's still light outside. Why don't we take a walk, and I can show you around a little."

"That would be great," Sam said, her green eyes shining.

The girls grabbed their sweaters and headed outside. First, Amy took Sam by the park, and then they walked through the center of town. It wasn't far to the middle school, so the girls went over there, too.

"It's so much bigger than my school," Sam exclaimed.

Amy looked at the building fondly. "I guess we have a lot of fun here. Considering it's a school, of course."

When the girls arrived back at Amy's, they settled down to watch television. Since both girls liked the same shows, there was no problem about which ones to watch.

"I can't believe how much alike we are," Amy marveled.

"That's why we make such great pen pals." Sam smiled.

They were in the middle of watching a horror movie, when Amy heard a car pull into the driveway. "My parents must be home," she said.

Sam sat up straight. "Maybe you'd better go warn them."

"Good idea." Amy was starting to feel a little anxious herself. She didn't know how her mother and father would react to an unexpected houseguest.

Mr. and Mrs. Sutton were just coming through the back door when Amy greeted them. "Hi," she said nervously.

Mrs. Sutton leaned over and gave her daughter a kiss. "Hi, honey. I hope you didn't miss us too much."

"No, I've been busy," Amy muttered.

"What have you been doing?" Mr. Sutton asked.

Amy took a deep breath. "Well, actually, I've had company."

"Elizabeth?" Mrs. Sutton inquired.

"She was here earlier, but then I got a big surprise."

Mr. Sutton looked at her curiously. "What was that?"

"Sam came to spend the weekend."

Mr. and Mrs. Sutton looked at each other. "Who's Sam?" Mrs. Sutton asked.

"Samantha Williams, my pen pal."

Recognition dawned on Mr. Sutton's face. "From San Francisco?"

Mrs. Sutton looked upset. "Were we expecting her?"

"Well, actually, she wrote to tell us she was coming . . ." Amy said in a rush. "But the letter never arrived."

"I think we'd better talk to Samantha," Mrs. Sutton said. "Where is she?"

"Watching television," Amy answered sullenly. She hoped Sam wasn't about to be sent home.

Her parents hurried into the family room. Sam jumped to her feet as soon as she saw them. "Hello, Mr. and Mrs. Sutton," she said, giving them a big smile.

After shaking her hand, Mr. Sutton said, "Samantha, your visit is quite a surprise. When was all this decided, and why weren't we ever informed?"

"Well," Sam began, "I've been wanting to come and visit Amy for a long time, and we had a long weekend. My parents were going on a camping trip this weekend so I thought this would be a good time."

Amy looked at Sam with curiosity. Sam hadn't mentioned anything about a camping trip.

"I *did* write," Sam continued.

"But what did you think when you didn't get a reply?" Mrs. Sutton asked.

Sam looked uncomfortable. "I guess I thought it meant it was all right."

"And is that what your parents thought?"

Now Sam stared down at the floor. "I didn't really tell them I hadn't gotten an answer."

Mrs. Sutton looked a little surprised. "Oh, Samantha!"

"But she's here now," Amy broke in. "Can't she stay?"

"Perhaps we'd better call your parents and make sure this is all right with them," Mr. Sutton suggested.

"Oh, it is," Sam said quickly. "Besides, we can't call them. They're way up in Northern California. Out in the wilderness. That's why I came here. I don't like camping."

Mr. and Mrs. Sutton looked helplessly at each other. Finally, Mrs. Sutton said, "Well, as long as you're here, I suppose you can stay."

Mr. Sutton added, "We certainly can't send you home to an empty house."

A cheer erupted from both girls.

"We're both going to be very busy this weekend," Mrs. Sutton warned. "So you two will have to keep yourselves occupied."

"That's all right," Amy said. "I don't even know how we're going to fit everything in." She threw her arms around Sam. "This is going to be great!"

As soon as Amy got up the next morning, she telephoned Elizabeth. "Can I come over?" she asked.

"Now?" Elizabeth asked, sounding sleepy.

"Well, right after breakfast," Amy relented.

"Sure, but what's going on?"

"I have a wonderful surprise for you," Amy said enthusiastically.

"What is it?" Elizabeth demanded.

"You'll find out, but I'll give you a clue—it was something we were wondering about just yesterday."

By the time Amy knocked at the Wakefields' front door, Elizabeth was waiting for her arrival with great anticipation. She didn't know exactly what she was expecting, but it certainly wasn't Samantha Williams. "It's nice to meet you, Samantha," Elizabeth said in surprise. "What a coincidence!"

"I know—isn't it amazing?" Sam said with a dazzling smile. "Call me Sam. All my friends back home do."

"OK, Sam, why don't we go out on the patio," Elizabeth said. "You can meet my sister, Jessica."

Amy made a face at Sam behind Elizabeth's back. She had already told Sam what she thought of Jessica Wakefield.

After the introductions were made, Jessica

leaned back in her deck chair and slipped her sunglasses over her eyes. She obviously wasn't very interested in Amy Sutton's pen pal.

"Are you guys ready for the party tonight?" Amy asked.

"I am." Elizabeth giggled. "Jessica still has some shopping to do, though. She doesn't have *anything* to wear."

"Very funny, Elizabeth," Jessica said, turning over onto her stomach.

"Oh, no," Sam said. "I just realized I don't have anything to wear to a party."

"Don't worry," Elizabeth said right away. "You're about my size. I could lend you something."

"Elizabeth's got some great clothes," Amy said.

"That would be terrific," Sam said gratefully. "Are you sure you don't mind?"

"Mind?" Elizabeth laughed. "I lend my clothes out all the time." She looked over at Jessica, who didn't say a word. "Let's go upstairs."

"Great," Sam said enthusiastically.

"Jess, want to come?" Elizabeth called as they walked back inside.

Jessica idly waved her hand. "No thanks."

The last thing she wanted to do was help pick out clothes for Amy Sutton's drippy pen pal. Still, Jessica wished she had planned something more exciting for that morning. She could sit around the pool anytime.

"Hey, you're starting to look like a lobster." Steven's voice rang out across the patio.

Jessica raised her sunglasses and sat up straight. Then she examined her arms. When she was convinced she wasn't sunburned, Jessica glared at her brother. "Did you actually want something, Steven, or are you just practicing being annoying?"

Steven put on a hurt look. "I was only trying to help. Anyway, Mom asked if you want to come to the mall with us."

"How come you're going to the mall?" Jessica asked. "You don't like shopping."

"A couple of guys from the radio club are going to check out the broadcast booth that's being built for the Carlquist show."

Suddenly something occurred to Jessica. With his recent interest in the radio club, Steven might actually know Dave Carlquist. Casually she asked, "Is Dave going to be there?"

Steven shrugged. "I don't know. I just want to check things out."

Jessica thought for a moment. Dave could be at the mall right now. And if he was, maybe she could arrange for an introduction from Steven. "I guess I'll go," she said, hiding the excitement in her voice. She jumped up from her chair and announced, "I'll be ready in five minutes."

When they parked at the mall, Steven jumped out of the car. "I'll meet you back here in an hour," he said. "OK, Mom?"

Mrs. Wakefield nodded. "Sure. Meanwhile, Jessica and I will do some shopping."

Jessica didn't know what to do. She remembered the sweater she had seen the day before. If she showed it to her mother, maybe she would buy it for her. On the other hand, she didn't want to miss Dave Carlquist. Finally she decided she would compromise. She'd spend half an hour with her mother, and then she'd find Steven.

"I need some new shoes, Jessica," Mrs. Wakefield said as they walked into the mall. "Want to help me pick some out?"

"Sure, Mom," Jessica replied. "But first there's something I want to show you."

It wasn't hard to talk her mother into buying

the sweater just as long as she promised to pay
a little bit a week out of her allowance for the
next few weeks.

"Thanks, Mom. You're the best." Jessica
threw her arms around her mother.

"I'm glad to hear that." Mrs. Wakefield
laughed. "Now what about those shoes for me?"

"Can I meet you at the shoe store?" Jessica
asked. "There's a couple of stores I want to look
at."

"All right, dear," Mrs. Wakefield said. "I
should be there a while. You know how long it
takes me to find a pair I like."

As soon as her mother was inside the shoe
store, Jessica raced to the center of the mall
where the broadcast booth, now finished, was
attracting a good deal of attention. She wandered around until she spotted Steven talking to
a boy a little older than he was.

"Hi, Steven," Jessica said. She pointed to
the broadcast booth. "Hey, this looks terrific."

"Yeah, it is," Steven replied without paying
much attention to her. He went back to his
conversation and Jessica glanced at the boy with
him. He was tall and thin and was wearing
horn-rimmed glasses and a faded T-shirt. He
smiled shyly at Jessica.

"Did you find your friends?" Jessica asked.

"Only Buddy, here. This is my sister, Jessica. And Jess, this is—" Before Steven could finish his introduction, Jessica had turned away.

"Well, see you later then," she said. Disappointed, she trudged back to the shoe store. She'd come all the way out to the mall to meet the fabulous Dave Carlquist and the only person she'd seen was some boring-looking boy named Buddy. She decided it was a good thing she'd gotten the sweater, because it really would have been a wasted trip!

Four

◇

"How do I look?" Sam asked later that evening as she and Amy got ready for Lila's party.

"Great," Amy responded. "After all, you did a pretty good job of raiding Elizabeth's closet," she added with a giggle.

Sam whirled around in front of Amy's full-length mirror. "Stop teasing. She had plenty of other outfits to wear."

"You're right. And Elizabeth is always generous about lending her clothes."

Sam smoothed a tiny wrinkle out of the green checked blouse which she wore with a pair of Elizabeth's black pants. The blouse complemented Sam's red hair perfectly. Amy had loaned her a pair of small green square earrings that were the perfect finishing touch.

Amy stood behind Sam and peered into the mirror, too. She was wearing a flowered blouse, a white cable knit sweater and her brand-new jeans.

"You look good, too," Sam said, smiling at their reflection.

Amy turned away. "I hope so." She was kind of nervous about attending the party. She wanted to look her best, because she knew she'd be seeing Ken Matthews.

"We should be going," Sam said, glancing at her watch. "Doesn't the party start at seven?"

Amy made a face. "Yes, and it takes a while to get there."

"I don't care when we get there," Sam said gaily. "I'm just looking forward to going. It's been a long time since I've been to a party."

But when they got to Lila's front gate, Sam had an apprehensive look on her face.

"What's wrong?" Amy asked.

"I don't know," Sam said slowly. "It's just that there are going to be so many new people there."

Amy put her arm around Sam's shoulder. "Don't worry. You're going to be a big hit."

Sam straightened her shoulders and tried to look confident. "Sure I will."

"Well, we're great for each other's morale, anyway," Amy said with a laugh.

As they walked down the stone path, Sam looked at the large Georgian brick house set among formal gardens. "This is an amazing house, isn't it?"

"Wait until you see the inside. Lila is really rich. Her parents are divorced, and she lives with her father. He spoils her like crazy," Amy added.

"Wow," Sam said, looking around. "It must be nice to get so much attention."

Amy knocked at the door, and a moment later a housekeeper dressed in a black dress and a little white cap greeted them.

"Please go out to the patio. The guests are gathering there."

Sam was awestruck by the splendor of the house as she walked through to the patio.

When the girls got outside, the party was already in full swing. Groups of boys and girls stood around the brick patio that had a beautiful stone fountain in the center. Behind the patio was a swimming pool, surrounded by fragrant lemon trees.

"Wow! I thought the front yard was nice, but this is really something!" Sam exclaimed.

Amy hadn't been to Lila's for a long time, and she had forgotten just how impressive it was. Feeling slightly uncomfortable, Amy looked around for a group to join. She was glad to see that Elizabeth and Jessica were just coming onto the patio.

Jessica walked directly to a group of Unicorns, while Elizabeth came straight to Sam and Amy. "How long have you been here?" she asked.

"We just arrived," Amy answered.

"Did you say hello to Lila yet?"

Amy shook her head. She wasn't really looking forward to greeting Lila.

"Well, we might as well get it over with," Elizabeth said. "She's over there."

The trio dutifully walked over to Lila, who was standing with Jessica, Ellen Riteman, and Tamara Chase, an eighth-grade Unicorn. After saying hello, Amy introduced Sam. "She's my pen pal, and she arrived unexpectedly, yesterday," Amy said. "I didn't think you would mind if she came to the party, too."

"Oh, you didn't?" Lila's tone was icy as she gave Sam a skeptical once-over.

There was an awkward silence. Then Sam said, "You have a beautiful house, Lila. It reminds me of those mansions near San Francisco that you can take tours of."

Lila's stern expression softened. "Thanks. I made sure the gardeners worked extra hard to make the patio look nice."

Ellen turned toward the Unicorns, shutting out Elizabeth, Amy, and Sam. "When do you think Bruce is going to show up?"

"Let's go," Amy whispered, but Sam didn't budge.

"You go ahead. I'm going to stay and talk for a while."

Amy stared at her with surprise. "Are you sure?"

Sam nodded and moved closer to Jessica. Amy and Elizabeth looked at each other and shrugged. Then, leaving Sam with the Unicorns, they walked over to a cloth-covered table where a waiter was setting out cold drinks.

"Who's Bruce?" Sam asked brightly.

Jessica rolled her eyes. Who needed this dull friend of Amy's butting into the conversation? But Tamara politely told Sam that Bruce was the best-looking boy in the seventh grade.

"I have a friend like that," Sam said. "His mother's Glinda Paris."

"You know Glinda Paris's son?" Lila asked in surprise. Glinda Paris was one of the Unicorns' favorite TV stars.

"Well, it's a little more than just knowing him," Sam said modestly.

"You mean, he's your boyfriend?" Ellen demanded.

Sam gave a little shrug.

"I thought you lived in San Francisco," Jessica said skeptically.

"Just outside of it," Sam corrected. "So does Todd Paris. His parents are divorced, and he lives with his dad."

"What's San Francisco like?" Tamara asked with interest. "I've never been there."

"Oh, it's great," Sam said enthusiastically. She launched into a description of the city, telling the girls about exciting Fisherman's Wharf, the bustling downtown, and exotic Chinatown. By the time she was finished, most of the girls were wishing that they lived there. Except for Jessica, who didn't like all the attention the newcomer was getting.

Sam was telling them about Golden Gate

Park when she was interrupted by Janet How-ell, who said, "Lila, you're just standing here in the corner. Don't you want to talk to the rest of your guests?"

"In a minute," Lila said impatiently. "Sam's telling us about San Francisco."

"Her boyfriend is Glinda Paris's son," Ellen said importantly.

"Really?" Janet was impressed.

"Look," Jessica said. "They're starting to put out the food. Why don't we go get some?"

"All right," Lila agreed. "It's great stuff. Little hot dogs wrapped in croissants, and shrimp on toast. And while we're eating, Sam can tell us more about San Francisco."

"Look at them," Amy said to Elizabeth as they sat in a corner eating some of the delicious food. "The Unicorns aren't letting Sam out of their sight."

"She doesn't seem to mind," Elizabeth observed.

"Sam's just trying to be polite," Amy de-clared. "I doubt she's enjoying their company."

Elizabeth wasn't so sure. It looked as if Sam, laughing and smiling and surrounded by the Unicorns, was having a wonderful time.

A little while later, the festivities were at their noisiest. The Hot Heads were playing the latest songs and the yard was filled with people dancing. Over in one corner of the patio, an elaborate dessert table had been set out, with a huge chocolate cake as the centerpiece. Some of the boys were already lining up, plates in hand.

Elizabeth was just finishing a dance with Patrick Morris when Amy, looking upset, came up to her. "Can I see you for a minute?" she asked.

Elizabeth smiled apologetically at Patrick. "Sure." She stepped away from the crowd on the patio. "What's up?"

"Look at Sam."

Elizabeth glanced over to where Amy was pointing. At the far end of the patio Sam was dancing with Ken Matthews.

Elizabeth shrugged. "It looks like she's having a good time."

"That's the third time they've danced together," Amy said grimly.

Elizabeth could see how hurt her friend was. She patted Amy on the shoulder. "She probably doesn't know you like him."

"I told her all about him last night."

This surprised Elizabeth. "Sam wouldn't do something to deliberately hurt you, would she?" she asked.

"I don't know," Amy said helplessly. "I wouldn't have thought so."

"Maybe you should say something to her."

"I think I will." Determined, she walked over to Sam, who was following Ken to the dessert table. "Sam—" Amy began, but before she could say any more, Lila came up to them.

"Sam," she said, ignoring Amy, "some of the Unicorns are going to eat their desserts beside the pool. Why don't you sit with us?"

Sam acted as if Amy weren't there. "Great," she said enthusiastically. "Let me go get a piece of cake and I'll meet you over there."

When Sam walked away, Lila turned to Amy. Tossing her hair over her shoulder, she remarked, "I'm really surprised you and Sam are such good friends."

Amy tried to keep her tone even. "Why is that?"

Lila shrugged. "She's wonderful. It doesn't seem like you two would have much in common."

Before Amy could think of a reply, Lila hurried away to join the Unicorns.

"Did you get to talk to Sam?" Elizabeth asked, coming up behind Amy.

"No." Amy's voice was tinged with bitterness. "She was in too big a hurry to join the Unicorns."

"Why don't we forget about it for now and go get some cake?" Elizabeth suggested.

"I don't want to," Amy said. "I've had enough of this party. I want to go home."

"It's still early. Don't leave yet."

Amy shook her head. "My parents should be home now. I'm going to call and ask them to come pick us up."

She walked into the house and phoned her mother, who said she would be right over. Then she walked slowly toward the circle where Sam was sitting.

All the Unicorns were clustered around Sam, listening in fascination as she told stories about her horse, Little Bit. "I ride almost every day," she informed the girls, after she finished describing how beautiful Little Bit was.

"I had a horse once," Lila said, delicately wiping her fingers with a napkin. "It was a lot of work."

"You're right, but when you win first place with your horse, all the work seems worthwhile."

"You have?" Jessica asked.

"Yes, I was the blue-ribbon prizewinner at a local show. Riders from five stables in the area were competing."

Too bad I have to break up this cozy scene, Amy thought as she came up to the Unicorns. She boldly went over to Sam and said, "I'm sorry, but we have to go now."

"We do? Why?" Sam looked very disappointed.

"My mother is coming to get us," Amy replied, avoiding Sam's question.

"Don't leave yet," Tamara begged. "I want to hear more about the horse show."

"And you were going to tell us about meeting Glinda Paris," Ellen reminded her.

"But if Amy is leaving . . ." Sam began.

"Oh, it doesn't matter if she wants to go," Lila said, waving a hand toward Amy. "Somebody else's parents can take you back. Or my father's driver will."

Sam looked hopefully at Amy. "Do you think that would be all right with your mother? I really want to stay."

"Do whatever you want," Amy said curtly. "I'll see you at home."

Amy didn't even look for Elizabeth to say goodbye. All she wanted to do was leave. When she got to the front of the house, Mrs. Sutton was waiting for her at the curb. "Where's Sam?" she asked.

"Someone else will drop her off later."

Mrs. Sutton looked at her daughter with concern. "It is kind of early to be leaving the party. Are you feeling all right, Amy?"

"I'm all right, Mom." As the car pulled away, she turned to look at the Fowler house lit up in the dark night. Music and laughter could be heard. *Sure, I'm fine,* Amy thought, *considering this has been one of the worst nights of my life!*

Five

◈

The sun streamed through the window and shone in Jessica's eyes. Jessica closed her eyes tightly and pulled the covers over her head. Why hadn't she remembered to pull her curtains closed before she'd gone to bed? She had been so excited when she'd gotten home from Lila's party, she had tossed and turned for hours before finally falling asleep.

With a sigh, Jessica rolled over and looked at her clock. It was only seven-thirty. For a few minutes, she stared at the ceiling. Then she wrapped her pink and white comforter more tightly around her and thought about the party. It had been so much fun. She had danced with all the popular boys including Bruce Patman and Aaron Dallas. And the music was the best.

The only bad thing about the party had been Samantha Williams. "What was so great about her?" Jessica muttered to herself. The Unicorns weren't usually friendly to new girls, but they had been positively enthralled with Sam.

Well, it doesn't matter much, Jessica thought. *She'll be gone soon. Besides, I have much more important things to think about.* There was only one more day until the winner of the radio show contest would be announced.

" 'Teen Talk,' " she said out loud. That would be the perfect name for Dave Carlquist's show. "Teen Scene" was one of her other entries. Whoever was judging the contest would be sure to select one of her brilliant ideas. She snuggled under the cover some more and thought about the wonderful party at Jupiter. Lila's party would seem like a five-year-old's birthday party compared to that one.

Jessica could hear sounds coming from the kitchen. The barbecue was to be held the following day, and Jessica knew her mother still had a lot to do. *I guess I should help*, she thought, but she was just too tired.

Jessica yawned. Maybe she would go back to sleep for a little while. She could always help out later. Another half hour, that's all she'd sleep, and then she'd be raring to go. Before she could reach over and set her alarm clock, Jessica was fast asleep.

"Hey, sleepyhead, get out of bed." Elizabeth shook her twin's shoulder. "It's after ten."

Jessica sat up and rubbed her eyes. "Ten?"

"Almost ten-thirty."

Peering at her sister, Jessica asked, "What's that white stuff all over your face?"

"It's flour. I'm helping Mom make apple pies. I thought *you* were going to help, too," Elizabeth added.

Jessica didn't feel like baking, but she thought a piece of pie would make a great breakfast. She stepped out of bed and put on her bathrobe. "I'll be right down."

By the time she was dressed and on her way to the sunny, Spanish-tiled kitchen, Steven was already trying to talk Mrs. Wakefield into cutting into one of the pies.

"They're for tomorrow, Steven," she said, shaking her head.

"But tomorrow is so far away!" Steven said. "What if a stray dog comes to the house and devours them?"

"It may be hard for the dog to open the pantry door," Mrs. Wakefield said with a smile.

"You always make way too much food anyway, Mom," Jessica chimed in. "You're sure to have some pie left over, so we might as well have a piece or two now."

Steven looked at his sister with admiration. "For once, you and I seem to be on the same side."

"What do you say, Mom?" Jessica persisted.

"No, no, a thousand times no," Mrs. Wakefield said, laughing.

Mr. Wakefield walked into the kitchen. "It sounds like you're being interrogated, Alice, and won't divulge some state secret."

"I won't give these two any of my freshly-baked pies for breakfast," she said.

Mr. Wakefield stared dreamily into space. "It's been years since I've had one of your pies for breakfast."

"Have some cereal instead," Mrs. Wakefield suggested, offering him the box. "Elizabeth is in the car waiting for me to take her to the library. When we get home, I want to see my pies intact. Do you understand?"

There were reluctant nods from the trio.

"Ned, I'm holding you responsible," Mrs. Wakefield said to her husband. "Can I trust you?"

"I promise to protect your pies," Mr. Wakefield said solemnly.

"Good. Then I'm leaving."

As soon as Mrs. Wakefield was out the door, Steven said, "Come on, Dad, let's dig in."

Mr. Wakefield laughed. "There is no way, Steven, that I would break my promise. Here you go." He held out the box of cereal. "It's this or nothing."

Steven grumbled but he took the box and filled a bowl with cereal.

"So, what are you kids up to this morning?" Mr. Wakefield asked.

Jessica shrugged.

"Steven?"

"One of the guys from the radio club is coming over in a little while. I may run the board for the show from the Valley Mall tomorrow."

Jessica poured milk over her cereal. She was

dying to ask Steven all about Dave Carlquist, but she knew her questions would make her brother suspicious. He might even tell Dave Carlquist she had a crush on him, and that would be embarrassing. "All of my friends are going to watch the show live," she finally said cautiously.

"It should be fun," Steven said, setting down his orange juice. "They expect a lot of people at the mall." He glanced over at his sister. "Apparently the famous Dave Carlquist has lots of fans."

Jessica put her head down so Steven wouldn't see the blush climbing her cheeks. Changing the subject, she asked, "Do you know who won the contest to name the radio show?"

Steven shrugged. "I don't have anything to do with that. I think someone from the radio station is going to decide."

Jessica was relieved when Steven and Mr. Wakefield started talking about a fishing trip they were planning. "I guess I'll go call Lila," she said, carrying her bowl to the sink.

"You and Lila ought to get walkie-talkies. We'd save a fortune in phone bills. Right, Dad?" Steven said.

"Just don't talk too long," Mr. Wakefield

said mildly. "I have to make a few calls my-self."

"You might as well ask the sun not to shine," Steven snorted.

"Funny, Steven. I'll cut my phone calls short when you limit yourself to three meals a day." With a smirk aimed in his direction, Jessica got up and left the kitchen.

Flopping down on her bed with the phone pulled into her room, Jessica dialed Lila's number. After a number of rings, a sleepy voice answered, "Hello?"

"Lila, are you just getting up?"

"Mmm-hmm," Lila answered, her voice barely audible.

"I wanted to tell you how great the party was."

Lila perked up a little. "It was, wasn't it?"

Soon the two friends were discussing every detail of the party: the food, the music, who wore what, who danced with whom.

"What time did Sam finally leave?" Jessica asked.

"She was one of the last to go."

Jessica was going to make a comment about Sam overstaying her welcome, when Lila said, "She's really neat, don't you think?"

Jessica didn't like to argue with Lila. "She was all right, I guess."

"All right? She's terrific!"

"But, Lila, how great can she be if she's Amy Sutton's friend?"

"Oh, they don't really know each other," Lila assured Jessica. "I mean, they're just pen pals. I'm sure if Sam went to school with us, she would be hanging out with the Unicorns."

"Well, she doesn't go to school here," Jessica muttered, silently grateful that Sam lived hundreds of miles away.

"No, unfortunately, she doesn't." Then, after a short pause, Lila continued. "Actually, I was thinking of bringing her up for an honorary membership."

"You're kidding," Jessica said. "We've never had any honorary members before."

"But we should," Lila answered. "After all, kids in other parts of the country ought to know how great the Unicorns are."

"I guess," Jessica said glumly.

"What are you doing today?" Lila changed the subject as quickly as she had brought it up.

"I don't have any plans yet," Jessica said.

"Let's all meet at the Dairi Burger for lunch, then," Lila suggested.

Jessica twisted the phone cord around her wrist. "Sam, too?"

"Sure. I'll talk to some of the other girls and see if they want to make her an honorary member. Everyone loved Sam last night."

After saying goodbye, Jessica stayed in her room and thought for a while. She didn't want Sam in the Unicorns, but she knew Lila was right. Everyone else liked her. Jessica thought it wouldn't be much fun to go to the Dairi Burger and watch everyone make a big fuss over Sam but it would look strange if she didn't show up.

Hearing the distant sound of the radio playing, Jessica wandered downstairs into the family room. She expected to find Steven in his usual position, sprawled out on the couch. Instead, Buddy, the boy with the horn-rimmed glasses whom Jessica had seen with Steven at the mall, was sitting in a chair leafing through a magazine. Just as Jessica turned to leave, he said, "Oh, hello there."

"Hi," Jessica murmured.

"I'm waiting for Steven. I hope you don't mind that I turned on the radio."

Jessica shrugged. "No, I don't care."

"I'm waiting for an announcement." He glanced at his watch. "It's supposed to be on any minute."

Jessica was about to walk out when she heard Dave Carlquist's voice coming over the radio. "Hi," he began. "I'd like to tell you about something special that's happening tomorrow night." Dave cheerfully explained all about the new radio show whose first broadcast would come from the mall.

"I can hardly wait for tomorrow," Jessica said enthusiastically when the ad was over.

Buddy smiled. "You're going to the show?"

"I'm probably going to win the contest to name the show," Jessica exclaimed.

"Really?"

"I submitted ten great entries," Jessica boasted.

Before Buddy could answer, Steven walked into the room. "Well, what are you two having such a deep conversation about?"

"Oh, nothing," Jessica responded. She said goodbye to Buddy as she hurried out of the room.

With a sigh, she headed upstairs to her bedroom. She supposed she should get ready to meet Sam and the Unicorns even if it was going to be a perfectly awful afternoon.

*   *   *

Amy slammed the refrigerator shut and poured a glass of milk. She had been up for hours, but Sam was still asleep. *Well, that figures,* Amy thought bitterly. Sam must have come in at almost eleven. She certainly hadn't arrived home by the time Amy had gone to bed.

"Good morning, honey," Mr. Sutton said as he came into the kitchen. "Sam's not up yet?"

Amy shook her head and took a sip of milk.

"Your mother's working on the convention, but I have a free hour or so before I have to do some work," Mr. Sutton said. "I thought I might take you two for a drive. Maybe we'll go to Secca Lake."

"That would be nice," Amy said without much enthusiasm.

"Aren't you and Sam having a good time?" Mr. Sutton asked with concern.

Amy was too embarrassed to tell her father what was going on. She shrugged and said, "Sure, I guess so."

Her father looked at her closely, but all he said was, "I'm going to be out in the garage doing a few chores. Let me know when you're ready to go."

Amy was just putting her dishes in the sink when Sam came into the kitchen, yawning. "Good morning," she said.

Amy muttered hello.

"Wasn't that a great party last night?" Sam asked, sitting down at the kitchen table.

"Well, I know *you* had a good time," Amy said pointedly.

"Yeah. It was really something. What's on the agenda for today?"

"My father said he'd take us out for a ride."

"Oh, that'll be fun. Is there any chance we could see some of the kids?"

Amy knew just which kids Sam meant. Before she could reply, the phone rang. Amy picked up the receiver. It was Lila. After greeting Amy curtly, she asked, "Is Sam there?"

Without a word, Amy handed the receiver to Sam.

"Hi, Lila," Sam said excitedly. "That was such a great party last night."

"I know," Lila said. "Listen, a bunch of the Unicorns are getting together for lunch at the Dairi Burger. Can you meet us there around one?"

Sam glanced at Amy. "Do you mean both of us?"

"Well, actually, we just wanted you."

Amy couldn't hear what Lila's answer was, but she had a good idea. She looked down at her shoes. She had no desire to spend any time with the Unicorns, but her mother had insisted that Amy and Sam stick together today.

Sam put her hand over the mouthpiece. "Lila wants me to meet the Unicorns for lunch."

"My mother said she didn't want us going off separately," Amy said in a strained voice.

Sam nodded. "Look, it's got to be both of us," she informed Lila. Lila heaved a sigh. "Oh, well, I guess that will have to do."

"All right. We'll see you at one."

The moment Sam hung up, Amy burst out, "You're supposed to be visiting with *me*, not the Unicorns. I don't want to have anything to do with those girls."

Sam looked surprised. "I don't know why. They're a great group."

"How would you know?" Amy said angrily. "You've only been here one day. They're conceited, and they can be really mean."

"Oh, I think you're wrong about them, Amy," Sam said. "Those girls couldn't have been nicer to me last night."

Amy threw up her hands. "Maybe they were nice to you, but they've never been very friendly to me."

Sam went to the refrigerator and took out a carton of juice. "I guess we don't have to go to lunch," she said slowly.

"No. You're my guest. If that's how you want to spend the afternoon, we will," Amy said.

Sam brightened. "Thanks. And maybe this will be a good opportunity for you to get closer with Lila and the other girls."

"Oh, great," Amy said sarcastically. "I'm sure we'll all get to be the best of friends."

Amy and Sam barely spoke as Mr. Sutton drove out to Secca Lake. But despite the ride being so uncomfortable, Amy wished it would go on forever. Anything was better than having lunch with the Unicorns.

When they arrived at the Dairi Burger, Sweet Valley's local hamburger place, the Unicorns were already assembled at a table, chattering away. Sam eagerly joined them while Amy tagged behind.

Everyone happily greeted Sam and then said

a few weak hellos to Amy. The girls immediately began talking about the party, while Amy stared off into space.

Only Jessica seemed as unenthusiastic as Amy. She noticed that Sam kept bringing the conversation back to herself. No matter what subject came up, Sam put herself right in the middle of it. When Tamara Chase began talking about a trip she had taken to Hawaii the previous summer, Sam said, "My parents have a house in Hawaii."

"I didn't know that," Amy said, looking at her with amazement.

Sam fiddled with her straw. "Oh, yes. We got it last summer."

"What island is it on?" Tamara asked.

Sam looked flustered. "Island? Uh, it's in Hawaii."

"Oh, you mean it's on the big island of Hawaii," Tamara said. "There are five main islands, but you must know that. We stayed on Maui."

"Sure. Well, our house is on Hawaii."

It seemed a little strange to Jessica that Sam barely knew which island her house was on. She began to listen to the conversation more closely.

When Janet Howell mentioned that she was going to represent Sweet Valley in the district spelling bee, Sam said she had represented her school at a spelling bee in San Francisco. Yet Jessica distinctly remembered Sam laughing the night before about what a bad speller she was. Jessica looked around to see if anyone had caught that mistake, but no one else seemed to notice. Jessica began to wonder just how much of what Sam was telling them was true.

After the girls had finished their hamburgers, fries, and shakes, Lila leaned back in her chair and said, "Look, girls, Sam is wearing a purple T-shirt."

Sam looked down at her striped shirt. "Is there something wrong with it?" she asked worriedly.

The girls giggled. "No," Lila answered. "It's just that purple is the Unicorns' special color. We all try to wear something purple every day."

Sam looked closely at the girls. Sure enough, Lila had on a purple scarf, Janet's socks were lilac, and Jessica wore a necklace with a small violet charm hanging from it. Sam laughed. "You all do have something purple on."

"Yes, and the fact that you picked it is a good sign," Lila said.

"What do you mean?" Sam asked.

Lila looked around the table. Most of the girls nodded as she looked at them, and Janet said, "Go ahead, Lila."

"We were thinking about expanding the Unicorns," Lila began importantly.

"Really?" Sam asked with mounting excitement.

"And even though you don't live here," Lila continued, "we'd like to make you an honorary member."

"Really?" Sam exclaimed. All of the Unicorns nodded and smiled. Amy, who had been sitting silently for most of the conversation, never felt more miserable in her life.

"How much longer are you going to be in Sweet Valley?" Janet asked.

"I'm not sure," Sam said, blushing. She glanced at Amy and then she looked away.

"Well, let's have an official ceremony tomorrow at Jessica's barbecue," Lila said. "OK, Jess?"

Jessica shrugged. She didn't like the idea, but there wasn't much she could do. "OK," she said reluctantly.

"It's going to be such a big day tomorrow,"

Mary Wallace bubbled. "First the barbecue, then the radio show."

"You mentioned that yesterday," Sam said. "Tell me more about it."

Everyone began talking at once, explaining about Dave Carlquist's radio show and the contest to name it. "It sounds fabulous," Sam said, her eyes sparkling. "You know, we have a school radio show in San Francisco, and I'm a deejay on it."

"You are?" Ellen asked, her eyes wide.

"Oh, yes," Sam said confidently. "Let me tell you about it."

Amy sighed and settled back in her seat. It was going to be a long afternoon.

Six

◇

Elizabeth was on the patio putting the finishing touches on the decorations and laying the checked cloths on the picnic tables. She was happy to see it was such a beautiful day. It would have been terrible if it had rained on their barbecue.

Jessica was supposed to be helping her, but she had disappeared when Mrs. Wakefield announced that it was time to start setting up. That wasn't unusual. Jessica was well-known for hiding when there was work to be done.

As Elizabeth put the last decorations in place, Jessica appeared in the doorway.

"Good timing, Jess."

"I had something important to do, Lizzie,"

Jessica said. She surveyed the patio. "But you always do such a good job without me."

Elizabeth remained silent. She didn't want to start the day with an argument.

"The guests should be arriving soon," Jessica commented.

Elizabeth looked at her watch. "In a while."

"Which of your friends are coming?" Jessica asked.

"I only invited two people. Amy and Julie Porter, but she went away with her parents this weekend. So it's just going to be Amy. And Sam, of course."

"Lizzie," Jessica said thoughtfully, "what do you know about Amy's pen pal?"

Elizabeth looked at Jessica with surprise. "Not much, why?"

Jessica made herself comfortable on a lounge chair. "It seems like she's been everywhere and done everything."

"Well, maybe she has."

"I don't think so," Jessica said bluntly. "Sometimes she can't even remember her own stories. And there was something she said the other day . . ." Jessica's voice trailed off.

"What was that?" Elizabeth asked curiously.

Jessica shook her head. "Something about dating Glinda Paris's son. I read an article about Glinda Paris in one of Mom's magazines, and it mentioned her son. But I'm sure it said he was much younger than Sam. I've been trying to find the magazine, but I can't."

Elizabeth sat down next to her sister. "Do you mean Sam is stretching the truth a little bit? Is that so important?"

"Of course it is," Jessica said indignantly. "The Unicorns have asked her to be an honorary member. We can't let just anybody in."

"Oh, gosh, no," Elizabeth said sarcastically.

Jessica continued as if she hadn't heard Elizabeth's comment. "You know, if I could prove Sam was making up some of those stories, the girls would never let her in the club."

Elizabeth was silent. Samantha Williams seemed to be causing problems for everyone. The previous day Amy had been practically in tears after her lunch at the Dairi Burger. The Unicorns had ignored her, and when they got home, all Sam did was talk about how great they were. She even told Amy she felt sorry for her because she wasn't a Unicorn. The whole afternoon had been awful.

Elizabeth didn't know Sam very well, but the way Sam was treating Amy made Elizabeth angry. She decided she would help Jessica find that magazine.

"Do you remember when you read that article?" Elizabeth inquired.

Jessica shrugged. "About a month ago, I think. And I'm not even sure which magazine it was in."

"Mom keeps a stack of magazines on her night table. We could look there."

"OK. Let's check it out." Jessica ran toward the patio door. Then she stopped and turned toward Elizabeth. "Hey, why do you want to help me with this? You don't care about who gets into the Unicorns."

"No," Elizabeth admitted. "But I do care how Sam treats Amy."

The girls looked through all the magazines in Mrs. Wakefield's room, but they couldn't find the one that contained the article about Glinda Paris.

"There're a couple of other places Mom stashes her old magazines," Elizabeth said. Then she glanced at her watch. "But we don't have time to look now."

"You're right," Jessica agreed. "The barbecue will be starting any minute now."

The girls hurried downstairs. Guests were already arriving, and Mr. and Mrs. Wakefield stood at the door greeting them.

"Oh, here come Lila and Janet," Jessica said, hurrying off to join her friends. Elizabeth had already said hello to one of Steven's schoolmates, and was talking to several of her parents' friends when she saw Amy and Sam come in. She excused herself and walked over to say hello.

Amy and Sam were a study in contrasts. Sam looked positively glowing, while Amy's expression could only be described as glum. Elizabeth noted that Sam had borrowed a purple blouse that belonged to Amy. The first sign that she was going to be a Unicorn, Elizabeth guessed.

After giving Elizabeth a quick hello, Sam walked off in the direction of the Unicorns. Amy's gaze followed her.

"How's it going?" Elizabeth asked sympathetically.

"Oh, great," Amy said. "I spent last night listening to what a wonderful group of girls the Unicorns are, and this morning I had to rummage through my closet looking for something purple that Sam could wear."

Elizabeth shook her head. "You know, Amy, I'm really surprised about all this. You always told me how great Sam was. What happened?"

"I have no idea. Her letters were always so nice and friendly. But maybe people aren't the same in person as they are when they write." Amy shrugged helplessly.

Elizabeth led Amy to a circle of chairs where they could continue their conversation in private. "I've been talking to Jessica, and she says that Sam is always bragging."

"She sure is. You should have heard her yesterday at lunch. She even said her family has a house in Hawaii."

"Do they?"

"It's the first I've heard about it," Amy said. "But I suppose anything is possible."

Elizabeth leaned forward. "Well, Jessica thinks Sam is making up most of her stories."

"I had the same suspicion," Amy admitted. "I even asked Sam why she hadn't written me about all the stuff she's been talking about, but she just said she had forgotten to."

"Jessica is going to try and prove that Sam is lying," Elizabeth said bluntly.

Amy's eyes opened wide. "How?"

Briefly Elizabeth explained about the magazine article Jessica had read.

"Wow. That would be great," Amy said, her eyes glowing. She glanced over in Sam's direction. "As far as I'm concerned, Samantha Williams deserves to be put in her place."

More Unicorns had arrived at the party, and Sam was happily the center of attention once again. Janet had started telling the group a story about her father's new car, but Sam interrupted saying, "My dad just bought a Rolls Royce."

"A Rolls Royce!" Even Lila looked impressed.

"Yes, he's going to take my sister and me for a ride as soon as I get home."

"Your sister?" Ellen looked at her curiously. "Yesterday you said you were an only child."

Sam gave a nervous little laugh. "Oh, you must be mistaken. I have a younger sister."

"I heard you say you didn't have any brothers or sisters, too," Mary Wallace confirmed.

"Well, you know how it is. Sometimes, you wish you were an only child." Sam shrugged.

The Unicorns looked at one another. But

before anyone could say anything, Sam was off on another story, this time about the shopping spree she and her mother were going to go on when Sam got back to San Francisco.

"The shops in San Francisco are the best." Finally, she took a breath. "Jessica, can I use your bathroom?"

"Sure," Jessica said, giving her directions. The moment Sam was out of earshot, she said, "I don't know about you guys, but I'm getting a little tired of that girl."

Janet folded her arms and pursed her lips. "I am beginning to wonder how much of what she's telling us is true."

"Maybe we shouldn't have been quite so eager to ask her to join the Unicorns," Ellen added.

Since asking Sam to become an honorary member had been Lila's idea, the girls looked at her. It was obvious Lila didn't want to admit that she may have made a mistake.

"I don't see why you don't believe her," Lila said, frowning. "After all, I've done all kinds of wonderful things in my life. It's possible she could have a horse, and be an expert rider."

"*And* her father owns a Rolls Royce?" Ellen said skeptically.

"*Plus* she's a deejay back home?" Mary added.

"And don't forget the house in Hawaii," Jessica said. "Nobody's life is that perfect."

"Well, we don't have any proof that she's lying," Lila said. "And I don't think we should do anything until we do."

"How are we going to get proof?" Ellen asked.

Jessica was more determined than ever to find that magazine article. "Excuse me for a minute," she said to her friends. "I'll be right back. And maybe I'll bring some proof with me."

Jessica was rushing into the house when she bumped into Steven's friend Buddy. "So, Jessica," he said, smiling at her, "I guess I'll see you later tonight at the mall."

Jessica didn't have time to talk to this boy now. "Sure. I wouldn't miss it," she said quickly. Then she pushed past him and found Elizabeth piling relish and pickles on a hamburger.

"Come upstairs with me," Jessica hissed. "I just thought of where that magazine might be."

"Now?" Elizabeth asked.

"Yes."

Elizabeth put her hamburger down and followed her sister. As Jessica took the stairs two at a time, she called over her shoulder to Elizabeth, "I've got some magazines under my bed. You can help me look through them."

Under her bed! Elizabeth thought. Finding the magazines might take all day.

But for once, Jessica was able to find something in her room without a major search. "Here they are," she said triumphantly, pulling out a stack of magazines. She blew the dust off of the top one. "You look through these and see what you find."

Elizabeth was still leafing through the first magazine when Jessica called out in triumph. "This is it! I found the interview with Glinda Paris."

"Well, what does it say?" Elizabeth asked.

"It says Glinda Paris has a son and he's only nine years old! Sam said this kid is her boyfriend."

"It sure does say that," Elizabeth said, scanning the article.

"I'm going to show the other girls," Jessica said, leaping off the bed. "This is the proof I've been looking for."

Jessica made her way through the throng of people to where the Unicorns were sitting. As usual, Sam was chattering away, but Jessica imperiously said, "Could you leave us alone for a few minutes, Sam?"

Sam looked at Jessica nervously, then her face cleared. "Oh, you must want to discuss something about the induction ceremony."

"In a way," Jessica said noncommittally.

As soon as Sam was out of earshot, Jessica opened the magazine. "Look at this," she said. "Sam couldn't possibly be the girlfriend of Glinda Paris's son."

The girls huddled around the magazine. "Well?" Jessica said triumphantly when they had finished reading.

"You're right," Janet declared. "Sam would hardly be dating a boy that young."

"Maybe Glinda has another son," Mary suggested.

"It doesn't say one word about another son," Jessica protested. "I think Sam is just lying."

Lila folded her arms. "I don't think we should make our decision based only on this," she said.

"Why not?" Jessica demanded.

"Wait a minute, you two. I'll decide," Janet said, putting up a hand. "After all, I'm president of the Unicorns."

The girls waited while Janet thought for a minute.

"This is what we'll do," she said finally. "Let's make up a completely outrageous story and see if Sam goes along with it. If she does, we'll know she can't be trusted to tell the truth. Then we'll decide what to do with her. Now let's put our heads together and come up with something really good."

Sam stared at the Unicorns huddled together in a corner. They certainly looked serious. She wondered what the induction ceremony would be like. Would she have to do something special to get into the club, or could she just simply join?

Sam looked around. She felt funny standing there all alone. Finally she decided to get something to eat. She wandered over to the grill and put a hamburger on a paper plate.

She hoped she wasn't going to have to eat it by herself. Fortunately, Jessica appeared at her side just then and said, "Oh, good, you've got something. We're all going to eat now, so why don't you just grab a seat at our table, and we'll join you?"

"Did you finish your plans for me?" Sam asked hopefully.

Jessica smiled. "Sort of. We can talk about it after we eat."

"Great. I can hardly wait."

I wouldn't be too sure of that, Jessica thought to herself.

Seven

◇

It took a while for all the Unicorns to get their food. Hot dogs and hamburgers were piled on plates along with potato salad and fresh fruit. Since the apple pies were going fast, Jessica grabbed a whole pie and brought it to the Unicorns, table so there would be plenty for dessert.

Once they all made themselves comfortable, the conversation began. The girls started to talk about rock singers, and Jessica said, "Well, you know who I love . . ."

"Melody Power." Lila finished for her. She turned to Sam. "Jessica used to be a big Johnny Buck fan, but now all we hear is Melody, Melody, Melody."

Jessica smiled helplessly. "I just can't help it."

"I like her, too," Sam said eagerly.

"She has a new album," Jessica informed her.

"I know," Sam replied quickly. "I got it the first day it came out."

Making sure Sam wasn't looking, Ellen winked at Jessica. Then she turned back to Sam. "I heard Melody Power was just in San Francisco making a movie."

"Outside of San Francisco," Janet corrected. "In fact, it probably wasn't far from where you live, Sam."

Sam hesitated. Then she said, "Yes, a whole crew was up there."

"And Melody had some kind of an accident," Jessica said smoothly. "I think she tripped over a wire and had to go to the hospital."

"That's right," Sam said, more confident now. "It was pretty serious."

"So, you know about it," Jessica said.

"Sure. In fact, I brought her some flowers when she was there," Sam went on.

"Did you actually get to meet her?" Ellen asked, her voice full of excitement.

"Well, she was kind of out of it. All that pain medication," Sam said slowly. "But, yeah, I did say hello."

The Unicorns looked at one another. They had made up the whole story. As far as they knew, Melody Power wasn't making a movie in San Francisco or anywhere else. She had certainly never tripped over a wire and injured herself, either.

We caught you! Jessica thought to herself with satisfaction.

The Unicorns had decided that if Sam fell for their story, they would wait until after the barbecue to decide what to do about it. So they continued eating as if nothing had happened. Just as they finished the last piece of apple pie, Amy Sutton came up to the table.

"Sam, we have to be going now," she said.

"Right now?" Sam asked with disappointment.

"Yes," Amy said firmly. "I told my mother we'd be home by five. She's expecting us."

Sam looked at Jessica and the others. "All right. I'll see you guys later at the mall, right?"

"Sure," Jessica said.

"You never told me about the induction ceremony," Sam reminded them.

"Oh, we'll let you know about that tonight," Jessica assured her. "Don't worry," Jessica added. "We're going to come up with something really special."

"Great!" Sam said, smiling.

"Come on, Sam," Amy insisted. "I don't want to be late."

"All right, I'm coming," Sam said. "See you all later."

As soon as Sam was out of earshot, the girls started talking. "I can't believe it!" Janet exploded.

"She's a complete liar," Lila said.

"So it was one story after another," Ellen added.

"I can't believe I was taken in by her," Lila admitted bitterly. "But don't worry, we'll fix her now."

"How?" Ellen wanted to know. "We don't have much time to come up with a plan."

"We could tell some really horrible boy that Sam has a crush on him," Ellen suggested.

"That's no good," Lila said, twisting a napkin. "She'll be gone soon. She won't be around to be embarrassed."

"Anyway it's not bad enough," Janet pointed out. "We need something worse."

"I wish we could fly Melody Power here," Lila said. "Then she could tell Sam in person that she was never in the hospital."

Janet sighed. "Too bad that's impossible."

"Wait a minute," Jessica said, snapping her fingers. "I've got a great idea." She leaned back in her chair. "Sam bragged about being a dee-jay, right?"

"So?" Janet said.

"That was probably a lie, too," Mary said.

"Sure it was, but that'll be part of the fun," Jessica explained. "We'll call Sam and tell her that Dave Carlquist wants her to be on his radio show tonight. "We'll even say he wants to talk about the time she met Melody Power."

"She'll die!" Lila exclaimed.

"Right. She'll think she has to go on the radio and tell a bunch of lies," Jessica continued. "We can even tell her that Dave is a personal friend of Melody, and he wants to have a nice, long chat about her."

"But she won't really be on the show, will she?" Ellen asked, confused.

"No, of course not," Jessica said impatiently. "She'll go up to the booth, and he won't even know who she is. He'll tell her to get lost."

"Ooh, how humiliating," Ellen said with delight. "Right in front of a mall full of people, too."

"Just think how nervous she'll be until she figures out she's been tricked," Lila said with satisfaction.

"And once she does find out, then we'll tell her exactly what we think of her," Janet said firmly.

The girls were congratulating themselves on an excellent plan when Mrs. Wakefield came up to them. "Jessica, I don't mean to break up the party, but most of our other guests have left."

Jessica looked around. Except for a few of her parents' friends, the patio was empty.

"I could use some help cleaning up," Mrs. Wakefield said.

"OK. But, Mom, I have to make a phone call first."

Mrs. Wakefield sighed. "If you have to, go ahead. But hurry up. Don't forget you still want to get to the mall later."

"I couldn't forget that," Jessica said. "None of us could."

The Unicorns exchanged secret smiles.

"Come on, let's go call right now," said Janet.

"I think I should be the one to call Sam," Lila said. "I was the one who asked her to be in the club, and now I want to hear her squirm."

"All right," Jessica agreed, "but I want to listen in on the extension."

"So do I," Janet said.

"We all can," Jessica told them.

They hurried into the house. Lila dialed Amy's number from the phone in the hall, while the other girls listened on the extension in the kitchen. When Amy answered, Lila asked for Sam.

"Just a minute," Amy said, not very pleasantly. The Unicorns could hear her yell for Sam.

"Hi," Lila said smoothly when Sam answered.

"Oh, Lila, I'm glad you called," Sam said happily. "I just couldn't wait to hear what you have planned."

The girls in the kitchen had to stifle their giggles. Little did Sam know just what they had in mind.

"Well, we've decided that before you can become a Unicorn, you have to go through an initiation," Lila said.

There was silence on Sam's end of the phone.

"I don't think you'll mind," Lila continued easily. "It will give you a chance to show off a little."

"Show off?" Sam asked doubtfully.

"Now don't pretend to be shy," Lila said. "After all, you are a deejay in San Francisco, aren't you?"

"Well, sure."

"So we're going to arrange with Dave Carlquist for you to go on his show tonight."

There was a long pause. "But what would I do?" Sam asked in a faltering voice.

"Just talk."

"Talk about what?" The panic in Sam's voice was noticeable.

"For one thing, you can talk about Melody Power. We've told Dave all about how you met her in the hospital. I'm sure he'll want to ask you a lot of questions about that."

Again there was a silence on the other end of the phone.

"What's wrong?" Lila asked sharply.

"Uh, nothing."

"You do want to become a Unicorn, don't you?"

"Oh, sure I do. But maybe Dave Carlquist won't want me on his show," Sam said.

"Don't worry about that. One of the Unicorns knows Dave really well," Lila lied. "It's all fixed."

"Great," Sam said in a tiny voice.

"So we'll come by and pick you up," Lila said. "Start planning other things you want to talk about."

As soon as she hung up, Lila raced down the hall to the kitchen. "She fell for it," Lila whooped.

"Did you hear how nervous she sounded?" Jessica asked with a grin.

"I'll bet she's feeling pretty sick right now," Janet said.

"I can hardly wait till we get to the mall," Ellen added.

After the girls left, Jessica decided she'd better have a look in her closet. She wanted to make sure she had a clean blouse to wear with her pink checked shorts. It was going to be a big night. Not only was Sam going to get what she deserved, but Jessica was finally going to meet Dave Carlquist. He would probably call her up to the radio booth when he announced her as the winner of the contest, and then she'd be introduced to the crowd.

With her mind on the evening's plans, Jessica went into her bedroom. A moment later there was a knock on the door. Jessica looked up and saw Elizabeth, her arms folded and a serious look on her face. "Mom wanted me to remind you to help clean up," said Elizabeth.

"I'll be down in a minute," Jessica said airily as she started flipping through her closet.

"I have the feeling that something secret is happening here," Elizabeth continued. "What do you have planned for Sam?"

Jessica hesitated for a moment, then she told the whole story. After all, Elizabeth didn't like Sam, either. She had even helped Jessica find the magazine article about Glinda Paris.

Elizabeth sat down on the bed. "That sounds kind of cruel," she said in a troubled voice.

"You didn't seem too worried about Sam's feelings a little while ago," Jessica pointed out. "You even told me she was being mean to Amy."

"But I didn't think you were going to do something this elaborate," Elizabeth said.

"Come on, Elizabeth. You know she deserves it," Jessica insisted.

"But it's going to be such a public humiliation. A lot of people will hear Dave telling her to get lost."

Jessica shrugged. "How do you think Amy felt all weekend when Sam was ignoring her?"

Elizabeth was quiet for a minute. She wasn't the sort of person who liked to see people hurt. But Jessica was right—Sam hadn't treated Amy very nicely.

Jessica sat down next to her sister. "You're not thinking of telling Sam what's going on, are you, Lizzie?"

Elizabeth thought about it. "I guess not."

"It would ruin everything if you did. Besides, I bet if you asked Amy, she'd be glad we're doing this."

Elizabeth nodded slowly. "OK, Jess, I won't say anything to Sam."

Jessica gave her twin a hug. "I'm so glad, Lizzie. It's going to be an outrageous practical joke."

It is going to be outrageous, Elizabeth thought. But even though she had agreed to go along with it, she didn't think she'd find it all that funny.

*   *   *

"What's wrong?" Amy asked sharply as Sam came into the bedroom. Sam had suddenly gone pale, as if she were ill. "Oh, nothing," was all she said.

"Well, it's all right if you don't want to tell me," Amy said bitterly. "You haven't bothered to talk to me much all weekend."

Sam lay down on the bed and looked up at the ceiling. She wouldn't even know where to begin telling Amy her problems.

Still trying to keep her room neat after the big cleanup, Amy decided to put her clothes away. Angrily she shoved a sweater into a drawer and slammed it shut.

"Could you make a little less noise?" Sam asked, rubbing her forehead. "I'm getting a headache."

"I've had a headache for about three days now," Amy said bluntly. "By the way, when are you planning to go home?"

"Tomorrow, I guess." Sam didn't seem too sure, though.

"Don't you think you should call your parents? What time does your train leave?"

Sam rolled off the bed. "Why don't you leave me alone?" she asked sharply. "I'll be gone soon enough."

Amy was surprised. Despite the way she had ignored Amy all weekend, Sam had never actually been rude. Now, she was glaring at Amy, her face an angry red.

"I don't see why you have to be angry just because the Unicorns like me and not you," Sam spat out.

Amy refused to keep her feelings bottled up any longer. "That's not it at all. You were supposed to be *my* guest, Sam," she said. "Instead, you've been spending all your time with the Unicorns this weekend and ignoring me. You've been a terrible guest."

"You're just jealous," Sam shouted. "I can't help it if you're not popular."

"I *am* popular," Amy yelled back. "Just not with snobs like the Unicorns."

Mrs. Sutton appeared in the doorway. "Girls, what's going on in here?"

"Nothing," Amy said glumly. She was glad she had spoken her mind, but she didn't want her mother getting involved in the argument.

"I'm sorry, Mrs. Sutton," Sam said. "Don't worry, I'll be leaving tomorrow."

"I did want to talk to you about your travel plans," Mrs. Sutton said, concerned. "What time do you need to be at the train station?"

Sam tried to hold back the tears in her eyes. "Could I check my ticket later? I need to get ready to go to the mall now."

"Certainly, Sam," Mrs. Sutton said. "But as soon as you get back from the mall tonight, I want to straighten everything out. Why don't we call your parents later on and firm up your travel plans for tomorrow? I'll need to know what time you plan to leave."

That's something we all want to know, Amy thought to herself.

Eight

◇

Elizabeth was lost in thought as she walked over to Amy's house. She had promised Jessica she wouldn't tell Sam about the Unicorns' trick, but that didn't mean she couldn't discuss it with Amy. This didn't feel like something she should keep to herself.

"Hi, Elizabeth," Amy said glumly as she opened the door. "I suppose it's time to go to the mall. Sam and her buddies left a few minutes ago."

"You don't look very excited," Elizabeth commented as she stepped inside.

"I'm not sure I want to go."

Elizabeth followed Amy into the family room.

"But you've been looking forward to the Dave Carlquist show for days."

Amy flopped down on the couch. "I'd like to see it. But I'm not very excited about watching Sam get into the Unicorn Club. You should have heard her talking about it on the way home from your house. It sounded like she was going to be crowned queen."

"Well, the plans have changed," Elizabeth said uncomfortably, taking a seat across from her friend.

"Changed?" Amy frowned. "What do you mean?"

"I told you that Jessica thought Sam was making up a lot of the things she said?"

"Yes, and then you and Jessica brought down that magazine saying Glinda Paris's son was only nine. But the Unicorns were still being nice to Sam, even after they found out about it."

Elizabeth bit her lip. "That was all an act, Amy. They were just testing her. They made up a big story about Melody Power being in the hospital in San Francisco, and Sam fell for it. She said she went to visit her."

"No!"

"So then they decided to get even with

her." Elizabeth filled Amy in on the Unicorns'
plan for Sam.

"So that's why she acted so strangely after
she got Lila's phone call," Amy said thoughtfully. "She seemed really nervous, but she just
went off with the Unicorns when they came to
get her."

"It's a cruel plan. Do you think we should
do anything about it?" Elizabeth asked anxiously.

"Yes, I do." Amy nodded.

"What?" Elizabeth leaned forward.

"Stand around and laugh right along with
the Unicorns."

"Oh, Amy, do you really mean that?" Elizabeth asked, dismayed.

Amy leaned back against the couch. "Yes, I
do. I told you earlier, Elizabeth, I don't really
care what happens to Samantha Williams. She
thinks the Unicorns are such great girls. Now
she's going to find out just how mean they can
be. And if I can be there to watch the fun, so
much the better."

Elizabeth didn't like seeing the hard expression on Amy's face, but she realized her friend
had been deeply hurt by Sam. She didn't feel
right about letting the Unicorns go ahead with

such an awful trick, but she didn't know what to do.

Mrs. Sutton came into the room. "Hello, Elizabeth," she said. Then she turned to her daughter. "Amy, do you have Sam's home number somewhere?"

Amy pointed to the address book lying next to the telephone. "I think it's in there. Why?"

"I have a busy day at work tomorrow, and I'd like to find out what Sam's travel plans are," Mrs. Sutton said as she leafed through the book. "I was going to wait until she got back home to call, but I'm anxious to talk to her parents now."

Amy shrugged. "She could always take the bus to the train station. That's how she got here."

"I'm still not happy about that," Mrs. Sutton said, as she dialed the Williamses' number. "I don't know what her parents could have been thinking letting her travel all that way—hello, Mrs. Williams, this is Dyan Sutton, Amy's mother. I'm calling to see about Sam's trip home."

"The sooner the better," Amy muttered.

"What!" A shocked expression crossed Mrs. Sutton's face. "No, I had no idea. You must have been worried sick."

Elizabeth and Amy exchanged questioning looks, while Mrs. Sutton listened and nodded her head several times.

"I see. But why would she . . . oh, I'm sorry to hear that."

"Sorry to hear what?" Amy whispered, but her mother just waved her hand.

"Of course. Should we tell her you're coming?" Mrs. Sutton paused, and then said, "No, you're right. Well, we'll see you as soon as possible."

When she hung up the phone, Mrs. Sutton sat down on the couch next to Amy, looking stunned.

"What is it, Mom?" Amy asked, tugging at her arm.

Mrs. Sutton looked at her daughter, her expression serious. "Amy, you didn't know that Sam had run away from home, did you?"

"Run away! You're kidding!" Amy gasped.

"No, dear, I'm not. I can see that she didn't confide in you either," Mrs. Sutton said, taking Amy's hand.

"You mean Sam's parents had no idea where she was all weekend?" Elizabeth asked.

"No, and they have been frantic. The police

have already been called." Mrs. Sutton seemed to be trying to put the pieces together. "I thought Sam's story was a little odd, but I was so busy this weekend . . ." Her voice trailed off.

"Did she leave a note or anything?" Amy asked.

"Yes, but she didn't say where she was going. Her parents checked with all her friends and relatives, but they never thought of calling us."

"But why did she run away?" Elizabeth asked.

Mrs. Sutton sighed. "I didn't get many of the details, but apparently Sam's younger sister has been very ill, and no one has been paying any attention to Sam. That's what she said in the note—that she was going to find someone who was interested in her."

Elizabeth and Amy exchanged glances. No wonder Sam had taken such a liking to the Unicorns.

"What now?" Amy asked.

"Her parents are flying down immediately. But we agreed it was best not to let Sam know they're coming, or she might run away again."

"So you don't want us to say anything?" Elizabeth asked anxiously.

"No, don't say a word. Just proceed with your plans. By the time you get home, Sam's parents should be here."

Mrs. Sutton drove the girls to the mall. Elizabeth and Amy were dying to talk about what was going to happen during Dave Carlquist's show, but they knew it was better to wait until they were alone.

As soon as they were dropped off, Elizabeth said in a troubled voice, "We've got to do something, Amy."

Amy nodded. "With all that she's gone through, Sam would be devastated if she was embarrassed by Dave Carlquist."

"That poor girl," Elizabeth said, shaking her head. "By making up all those stories, she thought she could get some of the attention she's been missing. But now she's going to get some attention she doesn't want." Elizabeth looked around the busy mall. "Maybe I should just find Jessica and tell her to stop the plan."

"Do you think she would?" Amy asked doubtfully.

"I don't know," Elizabeth said. "She'd have to tell the other Unicorns, and one of them could say something to Sam—"

"And then she might run away again," Amy finished for her. "What a mess."

The girls walked to the center of the mall where a huge crowd had assembled by the broadcast booth.

"Do you see Sam anywhere?" Amy asked, peering through the crowd.

Elizabeth shook her head. "No."

Just then Elizabeth spotted Steven adjusting some wires in the booth. "Wait a minute," she said, turning quickly to Amy. "I have an idea."

"What?" Amy asked.

Elizabeth tugged at Amy's arm. "Come on, let's go talk to Steven. Maybe he can help us."

The girls hurried over to the booth.

"I don't know where Dave is," Steven said, "so don't ask me." He looked at his watch. "The show isn't starting for another fifteen minutes."

"We don't want to see Dave," Elizabeth said quickly.

"Well, you must be the only girls in this mall who don't. I've been shooing girls away from here all night. Including your dear twin, Jessica."

"Steven, we have something important to talk to you about," Elizabeth said seriously.

"Can't it wait until later?" he asked, tightening the connection of a cable.

"No," Elizabeth insisted.

Steven looked at his sister, and saw the urgency in her eyes. "All right," he said. "What's up?"

Elizabeth explained the problem. "So you see, it just wouldn't be right to upset Samantha now," she finished.

"It wouldn't," Steven agreed. "But I'm not sure what I can do about it."

"Oh, Steven," Elizabeth said, upset, "I thought you could think of some way to help us."

Steven was silent for a few moments. Then his face broke into a grin. "Maybe there *is* something I can do."

"What?" Amy asked excitedly.

Quickly Steven outlined his plan.

"Do you think Dave would help?" Elizabeth asked.

Steven patted his sister's shoulder. "Leave it to me."

*　　*　　*

Over near the food stalls, Sam was trying to force down the slice of pizza the Unicorns had bought for her, but she had no appetite.

"I can hardly wait to hear you on the air," Jessica said, taking a bite of her own slice.

"So it's all fixed?" Sam asked with resignation.

"Sure. We told you that already," Lila said.

"While he's playing his second record, you're supposed to go up and introduce yourself," Ellen informed her.

Janet smiled. "Just say something like, 'I'm that famous deejay from San Francisco, Samantha Williams.' "

"I'm not famous," Sam murmured.

"I thought you were," Jessica said.

Ellen leaned forward. "Yeah, didn't you tell us you were written up in the *San Francisco Chronicle?*"

Sam could feel her words coming back to haunt her. She was sorry now that she had told so many lies, but they had just come tumbling out.

It had all started so simply. It was easy to go from saying that she owned a horse, which was true, to telling the girls that she had won lots of blue ribbons. Everyone had been so impressed. And the more stories she told, the more the Unicorns seemed to like her. But now she was supposed to tell her stories in front of a mall full of people. Sam clenched her fists. She just didn't think she could do it.

"Is something wrong?" Jessica asked pleasantly.

"I guess I'm just a little nervous."

"But why?" Ellen asked. "After all, it's not as if appearing live on the radio is new to you. You've done this kind of thing lots of times, haven't you?"

The only thing Sam knew about radio was how to turn one on and off and switch the stations. "You know," she said hesitantly, "I'm not feeling very well."

The girls looked at one another. "Sam," Janet began, "as president of the Unicorns, I have to tell you, if you don't go through the initiation, you can't be in the club."

Sam sat silently. Meeting the Unicorns was the best thing that had happened to her in months. There was no way she wanted to give up her membership in the club. Somehow, she would just have to get up the nerve to get through the interview.

"So, do you think you're too sick to do it?" Janet persisted.

"No, I'll be all right," Sam said.

"Good." Lila beamed at the other girls.

Jessica looked at her watch. "We should be going. The show's going to start in a couple of minutes."

The girls got up to throw their plates into the trash can. Shakily, Sam got to her feet.

"Let's go," Jessica said, taking her arm. "We don't want to be late."

"It'll be so much fun to watch you," Lila added.

Samantha allowed herself to be led away. It was like being led off to the most horrible punishment in the world.

Nine

◇

The Valley Mall was normally busy during the evening hours, but tonight the place was as crowded as if there was going to be a rock concert. Everyone was eager to see Dave Carlquist.

As anxious as Jessica was to watch Sam get what she deserved, she wanted to get a good look at Dave, too. Along with the rest of her friends, she hurried toward the middle of the mall, where the show would take place.

When the girls got near the platform on which the broadcast booth stood, Sam pulled back a little, but Jessica tugged on her arm. "Let's get closer," she insisted.

"Which one is Dave?" Sam asked in a quivering voice as she looked at the stage.

Jessica hated to tell her she wasn't sure. Right now, there were several boys milling around the booth; Steven, Buddy, and a few others.

Before Jessica could say anything, Tamara piped up, "That boy over there. The one with the blue shirt. He's Dave Carlquist."

Jessica followed Tamara's pointing finger and then felt herself go weak. Tamara was pointing to Steven's friend Buddy. Jessica tried to keep her voice steady as she said, "I thought his name was Buddy."

"You're right," Tamara said. "Buddy is Dave's nickname."

"H-how do you know that?" Jessica asked.

Tamara looked at her strangely. "Our parents are friends."

Jessica wondered if Tamara could be mistaken, but when she looked more closely at the goings-on on the platform, Buddy, or Dave, was definitely the center of attention. Steven and the other boys were asking his advice, and he seemed to be in charge.

He looked different now. At the Wakefields',

Dave had just been a plain-looking guy in regular clothing, but now he was wearing a fringed cowboy shirt and black jeans. His hair was slicked back, and his glasses had disappeared. He definitely looked like a deejay now.

"Isn't he adorable?" Lila breathed.

He was, Jessica had to admit. She peered up at the stage. In fact, everything about Dave was terrific. Watching him move confidently around the platform, Jessica could have kicked herself for not talking to him when she'd had the chance. Why, she might have actually gotten to know him.

With embarrassment, Jessica remembered that, instead, she had been rude to him whenever their paths crossed. Dave would never want to get to know her now.

"Say," Ellen said, looking up at Dave. "Wasn't he at the barbecue?"

Jessica pretended to be nonchalant. "Yes, he was there."

"Well, why didn't you introduce us to him this afternoon?" Janet demanded.

Jessica had no intention of letting her friends know she had made such a gigantic mistake. "He asked me not to," she replied smoothly.

"You know, he just didn't want to be bothered before his big show."

Lila looked at her closely. "That's not like you, Jessica. Keeping a secret to yourself just isn't your style."

Before Lila could say any more, Jessica put her finger to her lips. "Shh, the show is about to start."

Dave stepped into the broadcast booth and put his earphones on his head. One of the other boys sat down next to him, holding a sheaf of papers in his hands. Steven was on the other side of the platform, helping out at the controls.

"Maybe I'd better not interrupt Dave during the show," Sam whispered. "He looks like he's going to be very busy."

"No," Lila insisted. "He's going to be waiting for you. We'll tell you when to go up to him."

Music began blaring through the mall. Dave adjusted his earphones and started talking into the microphone on the desk in front of him. "Hello, everybody. I'm Dave Carlquist, and we're broadcasting live from the Valley Mall, right here on KSVR."

The crowd in the mall started applauding

wildly, and Dave smiled down at them. "That's right, let's show the people at home how glad you are to be here."

Jessica sighed. Dave's voice was deep and smooth, just like when she listened to him at home on the little radio next to her bed. How could she actually have talked to Dave and not realized who he was?

"We've got a big show for you tonight," Dave continued. "We're going to play some great music, count down the hottest songs on the charts, and bring you some interesting interviews."

"That's you," Lila hissed, poking Sam in the side.

"And, of course, we're going to announce the winner of the contest to name this show." Dave chuckled. "I suggested 'The Dave Carlquist Show,' but I'm afraid the station manager told me to forget about it. We've had a lot of great entries, and the winner is going to get to throw an excellent party at the new teen club, Jupiter. Hope I'll be invited."

Oh, you will be, Jessica vowed silently.

"But before we do any of that, let's start out with a song. Here's Melody Power and 'Happy to Be With You'!" Dave turned a dial, and the song burst through the speakers.

The Unicorns turned to Sam. "Well, it won't be long now," Janet said with satisfaction.

"You don't look very well, Sam," Lila said with mock concern. "I guess you were right about starting to get sick."

Sam didn't say a word. She just wanted to disappear. At least concentrating on the radio show would keep her from thinking about something worse, like what was going to happen tomorrow when she was supposed to go home. Sam knew she couldn't stay in Sweet Valley, but she wasn't going back to San Francisco. Her parents wouldn't care anyway, she thought bitterly.

For a moment fear clutched at her heart. It was scary to think about being on her own. But with determination, Sam put her situation out of her mind. She'd have plenty of time to make her plans after the show was over.

The radio show passed as if it were a dream. Sam knew she was supposed to be listening for the second song to start, so she could go up to Dave Carlquist, but she hardly paid attention at all. The Unicorns would make sure she wouldn't miss her interview.

Instead, she tried to recall the story she had told about Melody Power, but she couldn't remember all the details. All her lies were closing in on her.

Suddenly Sam thought she heard her name being called over the speakers. Her eyes wide, she turned to Jessica. "Are they calling me?"

But Jessica and the others were just as surprised as Sam was. *What in the world was Dave doing, asking for Samantha Williams to come up from the audience?* Jessica thought frantically. How did he even know who she was? He was supposed to ignore her, not welcome her!

"I'd better go," Sam said anxiously.

The Unicorns just stared at her. Why were they looking at her like that? Sam wondered. Something about this wasn't right.

Meanwhile Dave was telling the audience, "While we wait for Samantha Williams to come up here for a little chat, let's play a few commercials."

Sam hesitantly began walking toward the stage. She expected the Unicorns to come with her, but when she turned back to look at them, they were all standing around in amazement.

As she pushed toward the platform, Elizabeth and Amy appeared at her side. "It's going to be all right," Amy whispered to her. "Don't worry," Elizabeth said. "You won't have to make up any more stories."

Sam bit her lip. How did Elizabeth and Amy know about her lies? This was all very confusing, but at least they had told her not to worry. As Dave Carlquist leaned over to help her up onto the platform, Sam hoped with all her heart they were right.

With the commercials still playing in the background, Dave pulled out a chair for Sam, and gave her a pair of headphones. "Are you nervous?" he asked.

Sam nodded.

"Don't be. Just answer my questions. Pretend you're talking to me and me alone."

Sam was relieved to see Dave's smile was friendly, and the expression in his hazel eyes was caring. Maybe this wasn't going to be so bad after all, she thought.

"So, here we are back on the air, with a visitor to our town, Samantha Williams," Dave said into the microphone. "Sam, what do you think of Sweet Valley?"

Sam cleared her throat and focused on Dave

as if he were the only person in the huge mall. "It's very nice."

Dave looked at her as if he was expecting more, so she added, "The weather is beautiful."

Dave laughed. "That's what we're known for. I guess it's a little different up in San Francisco."

"It sure is. It can get really cold." Sam decided to attempt a little joke. "As a matter of fact, some people say the coldest winter they ever spent was a summer in San Francisco." When a titter went through the crowd, Sam was delighted. Suddenly, she felt a lot more comfortable.

In the audience, Amy whispered to Elizabeth with relief, "It's going really well."

Elizabeth looked through the crowd to where her sister was standing. "I'll bet the Unicorns can't believe this."

"Look at the expressions on their faces," Amy said, giggling. "I think they're in shock."

Sam was happy that her heart had stopped pounding. She felt almost normal now. Dave had asked her what her hobbies were, and Samantha had told him about riding and her horse, Little Bit. At least that was true. Sam realized how good it felt to talk to someone without lying.

"Well, Samantha. I'm sure my listeners enjoyed meeting you, and hearing what a visitor thinks of our town. Come back and visit us again soon. Now, let's listen to Johnny Buck's latest song. It's called 'Last Chance,' and it's really hot."

Dave switched off the mike and held out his hand. "Thanks for a good interview, Samantha."

"Thank you," Sam said gratefully. She stepped down off the platform and looked around for Jessica, Lila, and the others. They were standing in a tight little knot. Hesitantly, she walked over to them. "I thought it went pretty well—" she began.

Before she could say another word, Lila cut her off. "How did you get that interview?" she demanded.

"What do you mean?" Sam asked in confusion. "Didn't you arrange it?"

"No," Jessica informed her bluntly.

"But I thought it was part of the initiation."

The girls looked at each other. Maybe their plans had gone haywire, but they could still tell

Samantha Williams exactly what they thought of her.

"You weren't going to get into the Unicorns, Sam."

"But—"

Lila cut her off. "We found out about all your little lies."

Sam put her hand over her mouth.

"That's right, we know that you're not a deejay," Lila continued.

"And that you don't know Melody Power," Ellen added. "As a matter of fact, we made up that story about her being in the hospital to trap you, and you fell right into it."

Janet said, "You told one lie too many."

Sam was beginning to understand. "So Dave never really wanted me on his show," she said slowly. "He was supposed to tell me to get lost when I introduced myself, wasn't he?"

"That's right," Tamara said. "And what we want to know is how you got up there."

Sam could feel hot tears coming to her eyes. She had thought these girls were her friends. But how could they be? They had never gotten a chance to know the real Samantha Williams. She couldn't even really be angry that they had tried to get back at her once they had found out about her deceptions.

"You didn't answer Tamara's question," Jessica persisted.

Sam shrugged helplessly. "I don't know. He just called me up there." A picture of Elizabeth and Amy telling her not to worry flashed through her mind, but she didn't want to get them involved in this.

"Look, I'm sorry I lied to you about so many things," Sam began. "I thought—oh, never mind." With tears streaming down her face, Sam turned away from the Unicorns and stumbled blindly into the crowd.

As she began to run, she felt a hand reach out and grab her arm. She wiped away a tear and saw Amy standing in front of her.

"Where are you going?" Amy asked.

"I—I don't know."

"Why don't we go back and watch the rest of the show with Elizabeth?" Amy's voice was soft. "My mother will be coming to pick us up right after it's over."

Sam nodded, not knowing what else to do. When they joined Elizabeth, she asked quietly, "Why did you two arrange that interview?"

Elizabeth and Amy didn't know what to say.

"It didn't take much to figure out that you were responsible," Sam said.

Elizabeth cleared her throat. "The Unicorns wanted to get back at you. They were angry that they had fallen for your stories. When you went up to Dave, they thought he would kick you off the stage."

"I knew it was something like that," Sam said quietly.

"We decided it wasn't a very nice trick, so Steven fixed it with Dave to have him interview you for real."

Sam took a deep breath. "That was really nice of you, and I appreciate it, but I'm surprised."

"Why?" Amy asked.

"I haven't been a very good friend to you," Samantha said, looking steadily at Amy. "I wouldn't have blamed you if you'd let me walk right up to Dave and make a fool of myself."

There was no way Amy could explain more without telling Sam that she knew she'd run away from home. Amy looked over at Elizabeth helplessly. But Elizabeth just shook her head. She didn't know what to say, either.

Fortunately, the girls were distracted by Dave Carlquist's voice. "We're ready now, folks, for the announcement you've all been waiting for— the winner of the contest to name this show."

"Oh, this is it!" Elizabeth said, relieved at the interruption.

Dave smiled at the crowd. "As I said earlier, we had many fine entries. If I could, I'd give this show more than one name." He laughed. "But that might be confusing. So, from now on this show is going to be called 'The Awesome Hour.' "

Elizabeth clasped Amy's hand. "I don't believe it," she gasped.

"And the winner is . . . Elizabeth Wakefield."

Ten

◇

Amy threw her arms around Elizabeth. "You won!" she shrieked.

Samantha patted Elizabeth on the shoulder. "Good for you. Congratulations!"

Elizabeth was excited, but at the same time she knew how bad Jessica was probably feeling. Jessica had counted on winning the prize. She had even written out her guest list for the party at Jupiter. Elizabeth scanned the crowd, trying to find her sister.

Steven appeared at Elizabeth's side. "Dave wants to interview you, right now."

"Oh, I don't know . . . ," Elizabeth protested.

"No buts about it, star," Steven said. "You've

got to make an appearance." He steered her off toward the stage.

Elizabeth waved helplessly to her friends and allowed herself to be pushed onto the platform. She said a shy hello to Dave.

"The song is ending. Let's sit down," Dave said, directing her to a chair. "We're back," he said into the microphone, "and we're lucky enough to have our winner, Elizabeth Wakefield, right here with us. Elizabeth, how did you come up with the name, 'The Awesome Hour'?"

Elizabeth cleared her throat. "Well, I like writing and thinking about words. It just sort of came to me."

"Well, I like it." Dave smiled at her. "Now, tell me, what plans do you have for the party at Jupiter?"

Elizabeth looked down at a group of Unicorns standing in front of her. Jessica was biting her lip and looking very disappointed. Elizabeth knew at once what she had to do. "My twin sister, Jessica, and I are going to host the party together."

"You're going to share your prize with your sister?"

"Yes," Elizabeth said firmly. "She sent in a lot of entries, too."

Jessica grinned up at her, her face beaming.

"Well, it's sure going to be fun. And I thank you, Elizabeth, for picking out such a great name for my show."

When Elizabeth left the platform, Jessica ran up to her and threw her arms around her. "Thank you, thank you, Lizzie," she cried. "It's going to be great. I'm going to invite all the Unicorns, and Bruce Patman, of course . . ." Jessica began rattling off the names of everyone she wanted to have at the party. Elizabeth began to wonder whether there would be room for any of her friends, but she knew it was worth sharing the party to see her sister looking so happy.

"Jessica, I've got to go," Elizabeth said. She wanted to say goodbye to Sam.

"Sure, see you later," Jessica replied. She was already looking for the Unicorns. "I've got a lot of plans to make."

As she walked through the crowd, Elizabeth listened to Dave Carlquist announcing the end of his show. It was difficult to imagine that just a minute earlier her voice had filled the mall the way Dave's did.

Elizabeth finally spotted Amy and Sam near the exit and hurried over to them. "How did I sound?" Elizabeth asked anxiously.

"Great," Amy assured her.

"I hope I sounded as good," Sam added.

Amy glanced at her watch. "I guess we have to be going now. My mother will be waiting."

Elizabeth turned to Sam. "I'm going to get a ride home with one of Steven's friends so I won't be coming with you now. I guess you'll be leaving Sweet Valley tomorrow night?" she said.

Sam nodded. "It's been really nice meeting you, Elizabeth. I'm sorry we didn't get to spend more time with each other," she said wistfully.

"Next time," Elizabeth said, patting her arm.

"I hope so," Sam said sincerely. She waved goodbye as she and Amy walked toward the mall exit.

Mrs. Sutton was waiting for the girls in the parking lot, and as soon as Amy climbed into the car, she looked at her mother inquiringly. Mrs. Sutton nodded, and Amy knew that meant Mr. and Mrs. Williams had arrived.

Mrs. Sutton asked them about their evening, and the girls told her all about Dave's show. But neither of them mentioned Sam's interview on the air.

"Elizabeth won the contest to name Dave's show," Amy told her mother.

"That's nice," Mrs. Sutton said in a distracted voice. As they were pulling into the driveway, Mrs. Sutton turned toward Sam. "Sam, I don't want this to come as a shock to you when we walk into the house."

"What is it?" Sam asked, sounding puzzled.

"Your parents are here."

The color drained from Samantha's face. "But how did they? I mean—"

"I called them to check on your travel arrangements. And they told me you had run away. Sam, they were frantic."

"Oh, sure they were," Sam said bitterly.

Mrs. Sutton turned off the ignition. "It's not my place to discuss this with you, Samantha. All I can tell you is that your parents were very upset, and they are anxious to see you. Let's go inside and talk to them."

Sam clutched the handle of the car door. The thought of leaping out of the car and running away entered her mind, but she knew she wouldn't get very far.

"It'll be all right," Amy whispered sympathetically.

With a heavy sigh, Sam got out of the car. She wondered what kind of greeting she would receive from her parents. They were probably ready to punish her.

But the moment she opened the door, Mrs. Williams ran over to Sam and threw her arms around her. "Oh, Samantha. Thank goodness you're all right."

Mr. Williams was right behind her. "You scared us half to death, honey," he said, giving her a hug.

Mrs. Sutton patted Amy on the shoulder. "Let's leave them alone," she said. Reluctantly, Amy followed her mother into the kitchen.

Mrs. Williams led Samantha over to the couch. "Sam, how could you do such a thing? We've never been so scared," she said.

"Do you know we had the police out looking for you?" her father asked.

"The police?" Sam's eyes were wide. "But why did you call them? I left a note for you."

"Your note said you were running away

because no one ever paid any attention to you. But we had no idea where you were, or if you were all right," Mrs. Williams told her.

Mr. Williams shook his head. "You know awful things can happen to young people who run away. We were terrified."

Sam hung her head. "I didn't know you cared that much."

"Oh, Sam, how can you say that?" Mrs. Williams asked, her voice shaking. "We love you. I know that Emily's being ill has been difficult for you. We did have to spend a lot of time at the hospital, but we thought you understood that it couldn't be helped."

"But you missed everything," Sam said. "The horse show, and the Sixth-Grade Sing . . ." Tears came to Sam's eyes. "I was always the only one without any parents at those things."

Mr. and Mrs. Williams looked at each other. "You know it wasn't because we didn't want to be there, Sam," her father said.

Sam sniffed. "I know. I felt terrible about Emily, too. But I got so tired of being left out, and then I thought it would be easier if I wasn't there at all."

Mrs. Williams reached over and pulled Sam

to her. "I wish you could have talked to us about what you were going through, Samantha, before you took such a drastic step."

Sam fumbled around in her pocket for a tissue. She could feel her anger melting away. "I guess I should have. But all I wanted to do was get away."

Mrs. Williams took Sam by the shoulders and looked into her eyes. "I understand, honey. Promise me you'll never do anything like this again."

Sam began crying in earnest. "I won't, Mom. And I really am sorry. I'll never run away again."

Mr. Williams patted his daughter's hand. "We have some good news, Sam. Emily is coming home from the hospital."

Sam sat up straight. "She is? That means she's better!"

"Well, she's getting better," her father said. "And now that she's going to be back home with her family to help her, I'm sure she will recover completely."

"That's wonderful!" Sam said, throwing her arms around her father. Then she looked up at him, her eyes serious. "Dad, I know I've been selfish. Now that Emily is back, I'm going to make it up to her. I'm going to be the best big sister any girl ever had."

"Just be the best Samantha you can be," her father said.

Mrs. Williams kissed the top of her daughter's head. "I think we should leave now. We've been enough of a burden to Amy and the Suttons."

At the mention of Amy's name, Samantha hung her head. She realized that in addition to upsetting her parents, she had ruined Amy's weekend. "Mom," she said, looking up. "I've got to have a talk with Amy before we leave."

Mrs. Williams looked at her daughter quizzically, but she didn't press her for an explanation. "All right. We have some time before we need to leave for the airport."

Sam ran into the kitchen, where Amy was helping her mother fix coffee and sandwiches. "I thought you all might like something to eat before you get back to San Francisco," Mrs. Sutton said.

"Can I talk to Amy for a minute first?" Sam asked shyly.

"Certainly." Mrs. Sutton picked up the plate of sandwiches and the coffeepot and headed into the living room. "Why don't you girls stay in here and have your discussion. Then come and join us when you're ready."

For a few moments Sam and Amy just stood looking at each other. Finally, Sam said, "I owe you an apology, Amy. I was really awful this weekend."

Sam sat down on one of the kitchen chairs. "It's hard to explain, Amy, but for the longest time no one paid any attention to me. My parents were constantly running back and forth to the hospital, and when they were home, all they ever talked about was how my little sister, Emily, was doing."

"Weren't you worried, too?" Amy asked.

"Of course I was. But I got tired of always coming in second."

"I know how that feels," Amy said softly. "Lots of times my parents are busy with their work."

"When they didn't show up at my horse show last week, I decided to leave. I knew they'd check with all my friends in San Francisco, but I was counting on the fact that they wouldn't remember my pen pal."

"You got that right," Amy said.

Sam nodded. "And I was looking forward to seeing you, Amy. But then I got here, and the Unicorns were so . . ." Samantha groped for the right word.

"Terrific," Amy supplied for her.

"Yes, I guess so. Anyone could tell that they were the really popular group. When they started taking an interest in me, I liked it. All those girls wanting to hear what I thought and what I did with my time. At first I told them the truth, but after a while they seemed to be losing interest in me. So I began to make up stories, and then they liked me again."

"So you kept making up more stories."

Sam nodded. "And the Unicorns were really impressed—until they found out the truth."

"Yeah, that's one thing about the Unicorns, they don't like it when somebody makes fools of them."

"I found that out the hard way," Sam said ruefully. "I'm just grateful you and Elizabeth saved me before I really made a fool out of myself."

"We couldn't let that happen," Amy said simply.

Mrs. Sutton stuck her head into the kitchen.

"I hate to break this up, girls, but, Sam, your mother is anxious to get back home."

"We'll be right out, Mom," Amy said.

When Mrs. Sutton was gone, Sam said, "Amy, I'll understand if you don't want to be pen pals anymore."

Amy's face broke into a smile. "Are you kidding? I hope my pen pal is going to invite me to San Francisco."

"You'd come?" Sam asked in delight.

"Of course I'd come. Just don't introduce me to any girls like the Unicorns. They cause nothing but trouble," Amy said, laughing.

Sam laughed along with her. "Don't worry about that, pen pal. I'll stick to you like glue."

"Let's see, did I mention Peter Jeffries?" Jessica asked.

Jessica, Elizabeth, and Mary Wallace were sitting in the cafeteria discussing the party the twins were going to be having at Jupiter.

"Yes," Elizabeth said. "You've mentioned everyone at least twice. Besides, the club said they're booked up for at least a month. There's no point in doing all the party planning now."

Mary gazed out the window. "I hope I'll be here for it."

Jessica looked at her with surprise. "Where else would you be?"

Mary shrugged. "I don't know."

"What's wrong?" Elizabeth said with concern. Mary had had a difficult life, in and out of foster care, but now she was living with her real mother and her stepfather, and Elizabeth had thought things were going well for her.

"Aren't you getting along with your stepdad?" Jessica asked.

"Oh, he's great," Mary said with a bitter laugh. "It's my mother. She doesn't understand me at all."

Elizabeth leaned across the table. "You're not thinking of doing anything stupid, are you?" she asked bluntly.

Mary lowered her eyes. "I have thought about running away," she confessed.

"Don't do that," Jessica said. She looked helplessly at her sister. "Tell her, Lizzie."

"When Sam ran away, her parents were worried sick," Elizabeth said. "Running away is one of the most dangerous things you can do."

"Well, maybe I won't," Mary said, clenching her fists. "But I can't promise anything. If things don't change at home, I just don't know what I'll do!"

Is Mary going to run away from home?
Find out in Sweet Valley Twins #36,
MARY IS MISSING.